He held her gaze. Something unspoken fired between them. Something hot.

Something she should not, could not, would not act on.

When the door pinged she darted out, walked as fast as her silly shoes allowed down the corridor, fumbled in her clutch for the swipe card. But he was at her shoulder every step of the way.

'In a hurry?'

'Got to get my beauty sleep, you know.' She swiped the card. Red light. Swiped it again. Red. *Come on. Give me a break. Open up before I say or do something utterly stupid.*

'Need a hand?' He took the card from her fingers and swiped. 'There you go—first time lucky. If you need anything, just holler. As luck would have it, I'm right next door.'

She swallowed hard, closed the door behind him and breathed a silent goodnight. Then she switched the air-conditioning to freeze-your-socks-off and prayed she could get through working in close proximity with Pretty Boy and the weird sensations rippling through her body. Glancing over to the interconnecting door, she knew every ounce of her willpower would be tested to the limit.

Dear Reader

Thank you so much for picking up this book, my fourth for Mills & Boon® Medical Romance™.

The story is set during a fictional international rugby tournament, but much of the colour and background setting is from the very real experiences I had at the Rugby World Cup, recently held in New Zealand. I hope I have managed to encapsulate some of the excitement and atmosphere there was when the world came to party with us!

We met hero Zac, albeit briefly, in my first book, ONE MONTH TO BECOME A MUM, and my editor convinced me that he should have his own story. She was right, of course. Zac needed to find love—he just didn't know how!

Daniella, our reluctant heroine, was a delight to write, with her celebrity-obsessed family and her desire to put her mistakes firmly behind her. But she, too, didn't believe falling in love could be possible.

The essence of this book is about taking a chance and chasing your dreams. For Zac and Dani past events have made them cautious both when it comes to career choice and their love lives. But when their paths cross they have their beliefs challenged—in lots of sizzlingly interesting ways!

I hope you enjoy their journey—let me know at www.louisageorge.com or louisageorgeauthor@gmail.com!

Happy reading!

Louisa x

THE
LAST DOCTOR
SHE SHOULD
EVER DATE

BY
LOUISA GEORGE

To Annie Broadbent—thanks for the laughs and the love xx

First published in Great Britain 2013
by Mills & Boon, an imprint of Harlequin (UK) Limited.
Harlequin (UK) Limited, Eton House, 18-24 Paradise Road,
Richmond, Surrey TW9 1SR

© Louisa George 2013

ISBN: 978 0 263 23462 6

Har| |ible
and| |able
fore| |
lega| |

Prin
by (

A lifelong reader of most genres, **Louisa George** discovered romance novels later than most, but immediately fell in love with the intensity of emotion, the high drama and the family focus of Mills & Boon® Medical Romance™.

With a Bachelor's Degree in Communication, and a nursing qualification under her belt, writing Medical Romance seemed a natural progression, and the perfect combination of her two interests. And making things up is a great way to spend the day!

An English ex-pat, Louisa now lives north of Auckland, New Zealand, with her husband, two teenage sons and two male cats. Writing romance is her opportunity to covertly inject a hefty dose of pink into her heavily testosterone-dominated household. When she's not writing or researching Louisa loves to spend time with her family and friends, enjoys travelling, and adores great food. She's also hopelessly addicted to Zumba®.

CHAPTER ONE

DADDY, YOU OWE me. Big-time.

Daniella Danatello paused outside the ballroom ante-chamber, careful not to scuff her just-dried perfectly manicured fingernails on the ornate brass door handle. A fresh rush of nerves shivered through her.

Straightening her spine she allowed a deep breath of oxygen to infuse calm. *You can do this.*

This was just one of a hundred hurdles she'd have to jump over the next few weeks in full glare of the publicity she'd come to hate. The same publicity the rest of her family hungered for like addicts craved drugs. Maybe, once this ordeal was over and she'd proved her worth, her father would finally stop hounding her for not achieving his version of success. Although, the chances of that happening were highly unlikely.

She jammed her feet down in her ridiculous jewelled heels, patted her hair to make sure everything had stayed in place and flattened down the yards and yards of silver-grey silk. Hurdles were nothing. Whatever happened now she could cope with; she'd endured much worse.

Switching on her best smile she turned the door handle and waited for the barrage of camera flashes....

She wasn't disappointed.

'Dani? Dani Danatello? Is that you?'

'Dani Danatello! Hey! Miss Danatello, over here.'

'*New Zealand News*. A question…'

A wall of photographers and journalists stepped forward, the flashes almost blinding her. As she waited for her eyes to adjust she held a hand up to shield her face, then realised she had nothing to hide. They knew it all anyway.

'Dani! How do you think the Jets will do?'

'Dani? Do you have a heads-up on the final team pick?'

She drew in more oxygen as she'd been taught, breathed out slowly and steadied her voice. 'I'm sorry, I don't have any details about the team. You'll have to ask my father. Or Desere.' *Demure* Desere, her older sister, married to the team flanker. 'Or Deanna, maybe she'll talk to you, if you promise her a five-page spread.'

The youngest Danatello sister, *Dazzling* Deanna as the press dubbed her, engaged to the Jets' team tall boy The Lock, had sold an exclusive of their perfect hideaway proposal. Complete with close-ups of the moment Kyle had popped the question in a private hot tub overlooking the ocean. Surrounded by nothing but nature and birdsong, a stylist, photographer and make-up artist. *So romantic.*

Surprisingly Daddy hadn't been there, but he'd engineered the whole thing, just like he'd probably organised the phalanx of paparazzi here at the exclusive invitation-only charity ball. Davide Danatello, entrepreneur and chairman of the most successful rugby team in Auckland history, somehow always managed to mix his business with his daughters' pleasure. Keeping them close, and all but using them as bait to lure the world's best players to his team. And despite every attempt to the contrary now Dani was embroiled too.

'Come on, Dani! You must know the inside story.'

She fixed her plastic smile. 'No, my interest in the Jets is purely professional.'

'*Women's News.* Dani, you mean you're only interested in their bodies?'

'Obviously their bodies are of great interest to me.' No. That came out wrong. Her cheeks burnt. 'I mean, in a professional way.'

'So you haven't got your eye on anyone in particular? Not keen to be a WAG like your sisters?'

'Not at all.' Her stomach churned. 'No eyes on anyone.' And wouldn't again if she could help it.

Why the hell did it always turn so personal? She curled a stray lock of her hair round her finger as she fixed her gaze towards the ballroom. On the other side of the gilt-etched glass door people looked relaxed, chatting and laughing to the quiet strains of a string quartet. Ten strides along the red carpet. That's all it was, ten strides between chaos and calm.

She stepped her foot out to the accompaniment of more clicks and whirrs.

Nine strides. *Poise. Posture. Polite.* Her late mother's early grooming lessons came back to haunt her. Having been hounded by the press from the moment she was presented to them in a vintage christening gown she should have been able to deal with this intrusion. But she'd always hated the glare, the flashes, the raised harried voices. Hence the succession of photographs on various front pages of her, aged three, hiding behind her mother's skirt and, aged seven, sticking her tongue out. God, how she wished she was seven again.

Nearly over. The newshounds were just doing their job, then she could do hers. She exhaled, kept the smile, almost done. Her mojo was returning. She could do this. Could handle anything they threw at her.

'Dani! One more thing.'

'Yes?'

A microphone almost knocked her front teeth out as the

News hack barged forward. 'Tell us about rehab, Dani! Well and truly over your *exhaustion* now?'

'What—?' She turned and blinked into the mass of black lenses, her stomach clenched and her smile slipping. Gee, thanks, mate. Just in case there was anyone left in New Zealand who hadn't heard about the sordid details leading up to her stay at the Inner Sanctum. Words stuck in her throat. She wondered, briefly, how much force it would take to ram that microphone where the sun didn't shine.

Silence rippled around the room. All eyes bore into her.

'Dani? Any comment?'

Oh, yes. But far too rude to be broadcast to the watching millions only a satellite dish away.

Despite her promises to deal with that dark chapter in her life with humour and grace, she couldn't help but look at the reporter with derision.

'I feel great, thank you.' She wrapped the hair round and round her knuckle, brought it up to her mouth. 'We've all moved on. It was a long time ago.' Nearly five years, dammit.

Aware her shoulders had sagged Dani pulled herself straight and made for the door. Eight strides should do it.

'So, Dani, lucky for you the police dropped the charges. Very conveni—'

'Thank you, everyone. That's enough interrogation for one night.' A deep commanding voice and a firm arm turned her away from the cameras. But the flashes started up again, this time even more intensified.

Not surprising. Dani looked up at the man who'd moved in behind her. Even in stilettoes she only came up to his shoulder. She craned her neck to look into deep brown eyes and a genuine smile with a hint of a dimple in his left cheek. Floppy hair covered his forehead. Wide shoulders offered the chance to take refuge, and for a brief second the temptation to slide right on in threatened to overwhelm her. The flashes popped around them like firecrackers. And something strange popped and whizzed in her stomach too.

The man's voice oozed calm. 'Hang on to my arm and we'll be through in no time.'

'I'm fine, thank you,' she snapped back, through the faux smile and clenched teeth. She wouldn't be enchanted by a too-damned-sexy rugby player. No doubt another daddy set-up. 'I'm perfectly capable of doing this on my own.'

She'd resolved to get through the tournament ordeal on her own too, to do everything on her own. Alone was the way to go. Especially after her last failed fiancé fiasco. After everything...

But her feet wouldn't budge. *Great.* Rebellious feet and a rescue. She didn't need rescuing. Not by Adonis in a penguin suit, however gorgeous and strong he looked.

'Dani! Is this your new man?'

'Goodness, no!' She could see the screeching headlines now. *Dani Danatello's Dashing Date.* She shrugged his arm away but he held her tight. Close up she realised he wasn't a rugby player. Could have been with that toned physique— but he had perfect ears and no scars or rough edges. She'd memorised the player sheet on the flight and didn't recognise Pretty Boy here. She'd remember those eyes anywhere.

'Let's not argue in front of the children.' His whisper was a hot heat against her cheek, a strange sensation that sent shock waves rippling through her. She edged away, but he leaned in closer, his lips almost touching her ear. 'The secret to dealing with this lot is to imagine them all naked.'

'Eugh. Do I have to?' A bubble of laughter floated up her throat as she glanced at the beat-up *News* journalist who looked older than her grandfather. Then she turned back to her rescuer. *Imagine him naked.*

What? No.

An uninvited devil voice inside her head whispered, *Yes.*
What lay beneath that expensive suit?

She swallowed hard.

No. Heat seeped into her cheeks. Mentally reprimanding herself she stepped forward, catching the man's smile in profile. For all his hurry to save her he seemed to be lapping up the attention, shaking hands with a couple of the TV crews, waving towards the photographers squashed at the back. Irritation feathered down her spine. Another wannabe for the limelight. As if she hadn't already learnt her lesson with people using her to get to her father, or grab their fifteen minutes of fame. Or both.

He pressed a palm gently on the dip in her back and the irritation morphed into a tingle that zapped down her legs.

Then he winked conspiratorially. 'Well, the naked thing seems to work—you're not as rigid as you were ten seconds ago. Now try a real smile, Dani, it won't kill you. And stop chewing your hair—it'll all tie up in your stomach like a big fur ball.'

'What—?' Okay, so he knew her name because he'd have to have been deaf not to hear the paparazzi's shouting. But how did he know she chewed her hair? It had hardly reached her mouth, and she'd stopped that habit years ago anyway. 'I'm not chewing it.'

'Yes, you are. So stop it, drop your hand and smile. We don't want you coughing up on my shoes in front of these vultures. Now that would make a headline.'

'Your shoes are safe.'

'Thank God.' He laughed, a deep mellow sound that unfurled something in her gut. 'First day in my new job, I don't want to spend the evening hiding my feet.'

She angled her head to look at his feet encased in shiny black leather. Big. How did the saying go? Big feet, big...

She swallowed. Big socks. Big personality too. Who the hell was he?

With a flick of his hand the journalists parted like the Red Sea and he steered her through. 'You have to play them at their own game. Don't let them intimidate you.'

'I'm fine. It's just too hard to see past all those lights.'

'So don't look. Take my arm.'

Before she could refuse he'd looped her hand under his elbow and whisked her away from the glare. A few strides later and they were through the glass door into an oasis of calm. Crystal chandeliers glinted in soft light, the low hum of polite chatter reverberated gently around the room. Elegant dinner tables seating eight, bedecked in crisp white tablecloths and splashes of the Jets' scarlet, filled the room. New Zealand's finest had been invited to celebrate the glorious commencement of the tournament that would see Auckland Jets make rugby history. And she would play the most important role of her life to date, and hopefully win a place in her father's heart.

Trying to soak up the calm ambience she wriggled her arm out from Pretty Boy's. 'I can find my own way now.'

'At least let me see you to your table.'

'Don't you have somewhere you need to be?' Like a different continent?

'Sure...a dreary charity dinner, possibly meeting the new team physiotherapist, getting stuck, no doubt, in a discussion about muscles and tendons and things that could send me to sleep.'

He leaned forward and slipped the unruly lock of her hair over her shoulder. As he spoke he held her gaze. 'You, on the other hand, would keep me wide awake.'

She ignored the frisson of excitement she suddenly felt, the way her skin jumped at his touch or the soft-spoken words that caressed a deep part of her. He was a man, plain and simple. And right now, in the wake of desperate grasping Paul the Prat, men were the enemy.

To add insult to injury, Pretty Boy was probably something to do with the management, ergo something to do with her father. She scraped in a breath and stepped out of his reach. Pure irony that the first guy she'd had a physical reaction to since Paul was one of her father's lackeys. So off limits, and then some. And he was hitting on her.

She tried to bite back the smile that smoothed over her mouth, knew when it hit her eyes because his pupils flared too. 'You do know who I am?'

'Sure, you're Dani Danatello. One of Davide's daughters.'

'Aha.' She bit her bottom lip to stop the laugh and nodded. 'Which one?'

'That I don't know. First, third, sixth? How many does he have?'

She held up three fingers, noticed a chip in one nail already. Like that would have happened to Desere. 'Three, that we know of.'

'Your family's on the front pages so often I lose track. Although…you haven't been there for a while. I would have remembered.' Curiosity danced across his gaze. 'I heard out there with the press that you're the one who went to rehab. The one… Ah. Yes. That one. You've changed a bit. Hair not so long.' A smile spread across his damned perfect lips as he prepared to say what she'd been hearing for the past four years.

One day she'd be remembered for something other than a childish prank that had gone woefully wrong. One day she'd be able to walk down the street without the usual smart-mouthed retorts. She drew herself up to her full five-feet-four-and-a-half. Plus a lot more of stiletto. 'Okay, buster, get it over with.'

'What?'

'The damned headline. You know you want to.'

"Desperate Dani's Drunken Dare."'

She winced. *Desperate* Dani. Ouch.

He smiled, but it wasn't the usual leery response she got from men. There were flickers of warmth there too. 'And just look at you now. Mind you, you looked mighty fine naked in a public fountain on your birthday.' And there he had to go spoil it. 'Twenty-first, wasn't it?'

'Twenty-third. I was very drunk. And stupid.' And too wasted to care. But now she did. And so, obviously, did Daddy's lackey. The press had splashed her naked image across the front page to highlight the dangers of rich kids' party lifestyles and binge drinking. And, generally, to humiliate her father.

It had taken a lot to come back from that, for them both. Although the fraught relationship they'd developed since still stretched on a tight and often fraying thread. But she would change that, by the end of this tournament. 'Why does everyone have to remember it?'

'Because it was a heck of a picture. Dani Danatello riding a marble horse statue, soaking wet...literally bareback... magnificent.'

'Yes, yes. The famous Lady Godiva moment.'

He grinned but looked a little bemused.

'Lady Godiva? The woman who rode naked on horseback through a town to complain about taxes or something? Centuries ago?'

'Yeah, yeah, my dad's a history boffin, I know. Pure class.' His gaze shifted down to her décolletage, this time covered with silk and chiffon, not two thick blonde braids. One swift glance back at her face and he frowned. He touched her shoulder and looked into her eyes. She wanted to shake away from his fingers, but they were strangely comforting. Despite being her father's lackey there was something quietly honest about him.

Or was he like everyone else and hiding behind a veneer of trust? She couldn't trust her own reactions these days.

'Dani, we've all done things we regret. It's how you stand up again that counts. Everyone will forget in time.' He said the words softly, but with a firmness that told her he spoke from experience.

'Four years, and there's no evidence to the contrary. But I'm past caring.' Call it self-preservation but she'd long since decided to focus on her career and put her past behind her. Shame others hadn't.

She took a glass of water from a passing waiter and gulped it down knowing she should be walking away from this conversation, from this man, but somehow unable to do so. Pretty Boy was irritating and beguiling in equal measure, but there was also something more about him that intrigued her. For once she wanted to put the record straight; if she was going to be taken seriously everyone needed to know she'd grown. She would not let her past define who she had become. 'I've worked damned hard to be who I am today. Which is a whole lot different to the stupid celebrity brat back then. It's easy for you to say they'll forget. But really, have the media documented every single mistake you've ever made? Made an example out of you? Every time I try to stand up they knock me down. You'd know a lot about that, wouldn't you?'

'I know enough about failing in someone else's eyes. I know what it's like to let people down.' He stilled, his hand wrapped round the thick stub of a tumbler. Something behind his eyes shuttered down, the heat waned. She got the feeling again that he understood some part of what she'd endured. Then he came back to her. 'But no one's seen you for years.'

'And that's exactly how I want it. Where I live and what I do keeps me away from all this...' She flicked a swirl of her designer silk dress, let it drop. Thank God her sister had lent it to her, because it would have cost more than she could have afforded on her wages. Not that it bothered her. Money didn't mean a thing. 'This pretense.'

'It might appear like that to you, but many would give their right leg to be here rubbing shoulders with elite athletes, movie stars, New Zealand celebrities. Besides, isn't this how the world works—money, position, power?' The way his chest puffed and his jaw lifted told her he clearly loved it.

And she'd had enough to last her a lifetime. Knew how it skewered people, took them away from the things that mattered, like family, love, truth. 'Not my world.'

'Which is?'

When she didn't answer he followed up. 'So why come back now?'

'It's complicated.' Across the room her father beckoned her with the crook of his finger. Dani put her glass on the nearby table. 'I've got to speak to my dad.'

'Wait. I'd like to take you to dinner, Dani, after all this madness has finished. In a few weeks. If you're free.' He studied her reaction and she wondered whether he meant free as in nothing in her diary, or free as in available. Either way it didn't matter, she wouldn't be going.

He drew out his wallet, handed her a business card with one hand and with the other curled that same lock of her hair around his finger in a well-practised move. She'd bet any money he'd done that a thousand times to a thousand different women. He oozed charm and sex appeal and...experience. His voice smoothed over her; his gaze sent jolts of heat skittering through her abdomen testing her resolve. 'We have a no-sex rule for the tournament duration. The team and the management. It sucks, I know, but this job is important to me and I wouldn't want to be tempted...not until we've won.'

'Whoa. Rewind. I'm sorry...?' She held up her palm and raised her voice over the crescendo strains of *Moonlight Sonata*—it came to an abrupt end just as she spat her words out. *'You want to have sex with me?'*

Oh, God. Silence shivered around the room. Her heart thumped in her too-tight bone bodice. For the second time in twenty minutes all eyes focused directly on her. For a woman shying away from the limelight things had taken a nasty turn. Unfortunately, the nearest rock happened to be the centrepiece of a large ornate fountain. And she had no inclination to crawl under it and recreate yet another fantasy for the spotty male teenagers of New Zealand.

She found a wobbly smile for the mayor and lady mayoress. Waved coyly to her father, whose face had turned a worrying shade of beetroot. Bowed gently to the lady in full Japanese formal dress.

Pretty Boy grinned and raised his water glass to a table of gaping rugby players, then tilted his head to one side as he watched her turn the colour of the Jets' strip. He was enjoying this. Damn him. 'Well, not immediately. Obviously. I thought we could work up to it. Maybe after the hors d'oeuvres...'

'I can't believe you just said that, Mr...whoever you are...' She turned the card over and read his name. 'Mr... Oh. *Dr* Zachary Price.' *Sports Doctor to Auckland Jets.*

Her heart sank. Pretty Boy was the team doctor? Not just some lackey, but the guy she'd be spending the next few weeks with, in close quarters.

And he wanted to sleep with her? Even more concerning, she had the distinct notion her wayward hormones thought the feeling was mutual. She kept her voice raised, just so he and the rest of the staring audience understood her sentiment. Loud and Clear. 'I'm sorry, Dr Price, but I wouldn't have sex with you if you were the last person on earth.'

CHAPTER TWO

'I'll take that as a no, then.' *Or at least a not yet.* Still holding the now empty tumbler Zac shrugged as his eyes followed the delectable Dani in her clinging smoky-silver dress. She stalked across the room to her father, her back rigid, her footsteps staccato.

Confusion warred with amusement. Truth was, after her outburst his interest in her had spiked, not deflated as she'd hoped—intrigued, maybe. Aroused, definitely.

But he'd had a lucky break there. It had been a stupid idea asking her out to dinner. His usual type of woman was independent and aloof, a woman he could walk away from, not half-frightened confused debutantes. And as a proud member of the serial daters club he liked to establish rules at the outset. Number one: no strings.

Number two: no commitment.

Number three: no meeting the parents. Okay, they all added up to the same thing, but it always worked out fine.

Getting close to people? No—he didn't do that. Not any more. It only brought with it a major dose of guilt when things went haywire and from his experience things always went haywire. He scuffed a hand through his hair and let the painful memories roll over him before he filed them back in the corners of his heart.

A few more things he'd learned, though; never give more

of yourself than you have to. Never make promises you can't keep. And never get involved with someone who wanted for ever. Because he just couldn't give it. For ever meant someone relying on him and Zac had a track record of letting people down in the most devastating of ways.

Dani—well, she had for ever written all over her creamy skin, designer gown and manicured nails. For ever, and high maintenance. Two things that instantly sounded warning bells.

Matt, the team coach, sauntered over and whistled. 'Hey, bro...was that...?'

'Lady Godiva. Yes.' As he said the silly nickname that had been bandied around by the press following her arrest, Zac felt a sudden and unexpected need to defend her. For the second time tonight. God, he needed to concentrate on this new job. That was what he'd gambled his safe career and family relationships on. Not to lose focus on some girl who he'd be better keeping away from.

But for all her bravado he'd seen behind Dani's spirited act. There were barriers in her eyes that kept everyone at bay and seemed to intensify when she looked at him. Given different circumstances it might have been fun to see how far he could penetrate those barriers; he'd always been one for a challenge. But not with Dani. He sensed she'd been hurt; he'd seen it in action with those facile headlines. 'But don't ever call her that. It was a long time ago but it still smarts.'

'Noted. Shame she's lost the braids, though. I liked them.'

'I said...'

'Okay. Pull your head in.' Matt's eyes widened. 'You're dicing with death there, Doc. You know Danatello's tournament rules. No drugs, no alcohol, no bawdy behaviour. *No sex*. Especially not with the boss's daughter.'

Zac's eyes drifted back over to the smoky dress. The soft

skin he'd touched for the merest second. The blonde ringlet curls he could imagine decorating his pillow.

Reality check: she'd broken cardinal rule number three—she was Davide's daughter. Heck, he'd met the father before he'd even met the girl.

But he couldn't pretend there wasn't an attraction there. The four-week sex ban had only started this morning and it was doing strange things to his head already. 'You know, there's absolutely no evidence that sexual abstinence makes any difference an elite athlete's game. In fact, spending time with wives or girlfriends might even help morale.'

Matt grinned. 'Yeah, I got you, mate. I agree, and so does the wife.' His eyebrows rose. A kindred spirit, clearly. 'I don't see why management should have to abstain too. Davide's got this crazy idea from some article he read; no sex is supposed to keep the players hungry and high with testosterone. It's not proven at all, but are you going to tell him he's wrong on your first day? Don't forget what happened to Stewy.'

'Ah, Stewy. A difference of opinion? Yeah, right. Davide dumped Stewy because he dared to disagree with the game plan. But the boss obviously didn't think about the effect it would have on the team. Or me.' The physiotherapist had been sacked one day before the most important rugby tournament since the World Cup. Leaving Zac without a right-hand man and facing a lot of work between now and the opening ceremony in a few hours. 'There's a salutory lesson in keeping your mouth shut, but maybe if I blind him with medical science, he might listen to me.'

'Don't waste your breath.' Matt slapped him on the back. 'Davide Danatello doesn't care about science. He lives for Auckland Jets. It's not like your last job—here, Davide is chairman, major sponsor and boss. So, if you want to keep your job, embrace his sentiment.'

'My last job was voluntary. Having a salary is a whole different ball game, I need to keep on his side.' But he knew he was at the beck and call of a volatile investor. No decent medical structure. Rash decision-making based on gut reaction and no clinical evidence.

'Absolutely.' Matt shrugged. 'And for twenty-eight days you'll have no sex—whether it's with his daughter or not—and no arguing, Doc.'

'And now, no physio too...I'm holding out for some yeses. The list of nos is getting too depressing.' Zac groaned as he watched the Jets players taking their seats, all decked out in black tie and suits that hid the metres of sport strapping holding them together. 'Three quarters of them need some sort of massage or intensive therapy between matches to even get them on the pitch in one piece. With the best will in the world I can't do that single-handedly. I'm good, but I'm not that good.'

His gut tightened as he took his place at the table, nodding in greeting to the others as the MC called for order. One empty place remained next to him. Some unknowing sap had forgotten to remove the table-setting card for the missing physio. Just another minor irritation to add to the rest. It all seemed so...unprofessional.

Great. It was supposed to be every boy's dream, working for their favourite sports team. If the Jets won the tournament there'd be glory in abundance. But, if he stood his ground and fought Davide's irrationality with reason he'd be out of a job completely.

His heart sank and met his fading libido somewhere around his navel. No women. No sex, and surrounded by jokers. Not to mention he'd thrown his successful GP career over for this. Left his well-earning practice and the safety net of friends and scrap of family. The 'life's-too-short' lesson he'd learnt from Tom's accident was back to kick him in the butt. Today, life's-too-short was fast morphing into be-careful-what-you-wish-for.

Fly-by-night, his parents had called him, wastrel. Unreliable. And a whole host of other unsavoury things that boiled down to the fact that he'd disappointed them. Again. Tom must have thought the same too, once, but didn't have the guts to put it into words. Zac had a history of letting people down.

So whatever happened he couldn't fail.

As he once again pushed the painful memories away, he picked up the absent physio's place card and threw it into the centre of the table, nudging Matt on his right. 'I don't want some shonky rookie physio. Whoever Davide gets had better be good and he'd better be experienced. I haven't got time to explain things. I need action.' Zac shrugged and gestured towards the casualty line-up on the next table. 'I want these boys to win as much as anyone else does. There's a lot riding on this tournament.'

'He's on to it. He'll find someone.' Matt pulled out a crumpled sheet of paper. 'Here's tomorrow's timetable. Breakfast at six, media call, captain's run, injury clinic, then the bus to the opening ceremony and first game. It's going to be intense.' He shrugged. 'Cheer up, Doc. There'd be no time for sex anyway.'

Zac found a grin and tried to own it. 'Well, in my limited downtime I'll try to think of a unique way to use up those two thousand condoms I was given by one of the bronze tier sponsors.'

'Two thousand?' Matt spluttered into his sparkling water. 'Your reputation goes before you?'

'They're for the players—got to keep them safe, you know. Sports doctoring's about the whole body, not just muscles.' He grinned and leaned back in his chair, his hands clasped behind his head. 'But hey, what can I say? My reputation's done me no harm in the past. I like women. So what? It's not a crime. All work and all play makes Zac a happy man.'

'What makes Zac a happy man? Oh, don't tell me, I think I know already.' Dani's polite voice drifted over him along with that expensive perfume that had him turning instinctively towards her. She stood next to the empty chair and looked for all intents like she was going to sit in it. Surely that wouldn't go down well with Davide Danatello.

Zac opened his mouth to speak but she beat him to it.

'Shame about the ban though. And the public rejection.'

'Dani, how nice to see you.' He stood immediately. Noticing for the tenth time her eyelids were covered in a shimmering gold that made her blue eyes shine. It was dazzling. She was dazzling. And obviously rattled. Not a good sign if their last conversation was anything to go by. He determined to keep both his trousers and his dirty mouth zipped. 'The keynote's on in a minute. Shouldn't you be getting to your seat?'

'I am.' She offered him a bitter smile and the temperature in their corner of the room dropped ten degrees. She nodded at the rest of the guys at the table. 'Evening, gentlemen.'

Murmured responses and wide eyes greeted her. And every single one of them straightened their shoulders and stared at her cleavage like rabbits caught in headlights. He knew exactly what was going on in their puerile brains, and it involved blonde braids and a horse.

He felt duty bound to shield her from their ogling but luckily the lights began to dim and their attention diverted to the stage. 'Er...I think that chair is taken,' Zac whispered as she sat down in it. 'Or it will be.' Hopefully soon, if Davide pulled his finger out.

'Oh, yes.' Her voice was determined and definitive. 'It is. We haven't been properly introduced, Dr Price.' She stuck out her perfectly polished hand and flashed that false smile she'd used for the hacks outside. 'I'm Daniella, the new team physio.'

Hard to imagine that the moth around the paparazzi flames would be lost for words, but Dani watched as Zac frowned, lifted a glass and downed the contents. If she hadn't seen the light in his eyes dimmed as she'd admitted why she was really here she'd have found the scenario amusing.

Once she would have cared, but she had determined to rise above what people thought of her. She was here to work whether he liked it or not. Building friendships wasn't in the job description.

She dredged up her impartial mask, listened politely to her father welcoming the international dignitaries and guests, watched a seemingly never-ending line of famous ex-players extol their excitement about the tournament and managed to pick at a few morsels of finest New Zealand lamb and a kiwifruit soufflé. All the while hyper-aware of Zac's poker-straight back, the tight line of his jaw and the distinct air of disappointment. Having grown up in the shadow of it, she recognised it well.

Dinner finished and the band started up. Suddenly finding herself the only one on the crowded table not in a conversation she fiddled with the crockery. Curled her fingers in her hair. Tapped her leg to the beat.

The whole team set-up felt like an old boys' club, and she definitely hadn't been made welcome. She swallowed the stirrings of anger behind her smile and sneaked a look at Pretty Boy.

He'd undone his tie so it hung round his neck. His white starched shirt was open at the collar, one arm slouched over the back of his chair. Everything about him screamed success and ease and he looked like he'd fit in anywhere, had the kind of charm and grace her father had tried to master and yet had never managed.

But his dark eyes burnt with indignation as he turned to her. 'So, jobs for the girls, is it?'

'I'm sorry?' The fleeting relief she'd felt at finally being spoken to dissolved. But she'd conquered a zillion worse challenges than him.

'Working for Daddy? Very convenient.'

'Oh, whoop-de-dee. Another man who won't take me seriously. Story of my life.' Sitting in silence was preferable, but his irritating challenge warranted an answer. 'Convenient, yes, because I was available at very short notice, not to mention my excellent qualifications and my experience.' And the emotional bribery. *You owe us this, Dani. After everything you put us through.* And she did. But what they'd all been through had been a direct result of their outrageous parenting skills. She stifled a laugh. Didn't skills usually mean doing something well?

'So, you are actually a physiotherapist?' He leaned closer and looked at her hands. Which made a positive change to the part of her body his gaze had been fixed on for most of the evening. 'With those nails?'

'For someone who gives the impression of being a real man about town you don't know much about women. They're false? Like you and your phoney niceness.' It felt really good to be honest. Although, the light shuttered down again in his eyes and for a second she regretted her sarcasm. A few times in their brief conversation she'd almost thought he was different to the other men she knew. Almost. But then he kept spoiling it. However, she had to work with him, no matter how much she didn't want to be here. She needed to remember her poise and her posture. Polite was harder to muster.

Running her finger round the rim of her glass she forced

a smile and tried to soften. 'I'm a good physiotherapist, actually. Seems all that private education did me some good after all. Graduated top of the class.'

He nodded, eyes focused, sharp. Scrutinising her, and not just her physical assets. 'With sports experience?'

'Of course. Oh, for goodness sake, get off your high horse.' Irritatingly, his pupils flared at the mention of horse. 'Did you quiz Matt like this? Or the massage guy?' He had the decency to look apologetic. 'No, I thought not. Not that it's any of your business, but I've been working as a physio for eight months. I deal almost exclusively in sports injury. And, okay, so I don't have the years of experience that Stewy had, but I know what I'm doing.'

She drew strength and pleasure from the shocked expression on his face as she continued, 'And I thought this whole thing was about teamwork. You know, I had this weird dream that we could all work together. Or is that just for the boys? Is it too hard for you to understand that a woman might actually be able to do the job too?'

'Whoa. Hold it right there. You can turn me down for sex, but don't ever accuse me of being a misogynist.' He held his palms up in self-defence; his eyebrows lifted with a look of indignation all mixed up with frustration. 'It's not the fact you're a woman. I have no problem with that at all. It's the fact you're Davide's daughter. Usually Danatello girls don't do paid work unless it's to grace the covers of magazines. I was surprised. You've got to admit it's a bit different to the, er, braids...' He gestured down his body to his chest as if he was holding two large balls, and grinned. 'And the fountain.'

At his woeful impression of her cleavage she grinned back. And just like that her anger whooshed out of her. For the first time since it had happened mention of the fountain incident had caused her to smile. 'I had to do something. I couldn't spend the rest of my life living off my parents, getting wasted, not using my brain. Although everyone said I was mad—or even more crazy—when I announced that I wanted to be a physio.'

'But why this? You could have done any number of charitable jobs? You don't need to work at all, surely?'

'You saw me out there with those media people. I hate the limelight. I don't want to be a WAG or an It girl—the only letters I want associated with my name are related to academic qualifications. BSc works for a start. And I love fixing people, the physicality of the job, the sports environment.' Apart from when they treated her like porcelain. Or worse, left her out of the conversation altogether. She shook her head. Did everyone think all she was fit for was baubles and beads and a photo shoot? 'Sadly, you're just like my father. You believe the hype and can't see past what you think you know about me. Nothing more than marriage fodder. If Daddy had his way I'd be shacked up with one of his team. Preferably the one he couldn't lure here without the unspoken promise of bedding his middle daughter. Lady Bloody Godiva.'

He gently reached out and moved her hair-wrapped finger away from her mouth. 'Don't.'

'Oh.' Again already? Hours of therapy wasted. But she only did it when she was wound up.

At his touch something strange and electric zinged through her body. Why was she nervous around him? Was it truly nerves? Or just a by-product of her frustration at coming back to the family fold, or was it something else entirely? Something she hadn't felt before. Something wild that put her on edge. Something she didn't know how to deal with. 'Is it such a crime to want to help people instead of screw them for everything they've got?'

He leaned back in his chair and looked at her. His eyes

were kind and warm. A tiny crease crinkled at the corner of his eyes as he smiled. 'I misjudged you. I'm sorry.'

'I'm used to it.'

'Well, you shouldn't be.'

'Welcome to the whacky world of the Danatellos.' She inhaled, then blew out a long slow breath. This displaced feeling would soon go; she was only here for a few short weeks, the craziness of the tournament. Then she could be back in her apartment, back to her lovely job. 'Whatever. I spent one long month in the Inner Sanctum facing a lot of demons. The only thing that made me feel better was time out chatting to the staff. People actually listened to what I wanted instead of dictating what I should do. But by the end I itched to stop talking and start doing something. One of the nurses mentioned her brother was a physio at a college, helping kids recover from their sports injuries. It seemed such a nice thing to do. So normal.'

His dimple appeared as he smiled and shrugged. 'Hey, I come from a long line of stuffy academics. I grew up on dusty geological digs and boarding school. What's normal?'

She laughed. This was normal. Talking, laughing, being the person she wanted to be. Being accepted, not judged. Even if it had taken a little time, and she still had a long way to go. 'Okay. Enough about me, and my boring story. Tell me about the condoms.'

He coughed, and spilled the water in the glass he was holding. 'You heard?'

Glad to get a reaction out of him she offered a napkin. 'I have superpower hearing. Watch out.'

He dabbed at the water, leaned back, crossed his feet at the ankles and gave her the most mischievous smile she'd seen in a decade. She almost swore that wicked dimple winked at her. 'Dani, I have superpower stamina. Hence the condoms. Watch out.'

A flash of heat inflamed the pit of her stomach and hit her cheeks in nanoseconds. The idea of him naked rebounded into her brain again. Along with the sudden idea of how good he'd look against her Egyptian cotton sheets.

No. She pressed a cool hand against her clammy neck.

She was no good at this flirting; being playful wasn't her thing. She'd perfected the art of aloof. Besides, flirting was off limits. He was off limits. Men were off limits. After Paul's heartbreaking betrayal she didn't want to think about trusting another man. But she didn't know what to do with the butterflies in her stomach or the raw energy she got from talking to Zac.

Glancing around the room she realised the music had stopped, waiters were clearing the last of the plates and most of the party goers had left. The players had been under strict orders for an early night. Even Daddy had gone. For some reason she knew it would be safer tucked up in her bed, alone, than spending any more time here with Zac Price. 'Okay. Well, I'm going to bed.'

His gaze moved away from her and scanned the emptying room. 'Good call. Looks like we're the last ones at the party. I'll walk you to the elevator.'

His exotic woody scent filled the air, reminding her of how close she'd been to him when he'd *saved* her from the press. The aroma was comforting and exciting at the same time, with undertones of something else—his own natural smell, which was heady, all male. And intoxicating.

'Which floor?' She reached out to the panel of buttons in the elevator, now wired at her body's strange and intense reaction to someone she barely knew, her hand shaking, as an intense pulse throbbed in the tiny enclosed space.

'Eleven.' He leaned forward and his hand brushed against hers as they went for the same number.

'Oh, me too.' Her voice cracked and she snatched her

hand away, shifted into the corner, as far away from him as she could possibly get.

'Apparently management are clustered in the same area.' A lazy sexy smile smothered his lips; he seemed so comfortable in his skin. She guessed that mouth had seduced many a hapless girl. Well, she wasn't going to be another of his conquests.

'That's cosy. But I suppose it helps for meetings and things.'

'Things…yes.' His eyes glinted. 'I'm rooming with Matt. You?'

'On my own.'

'Nice.' He held her gaze. Something unspoken fired between them. Something hot.

Something she should not, could not, would not, act on.

When the door pinged she darted out, walked as fast as her silly shoes allowed down the corridor, fumbled in her clutch for the swipe card. But he was at her shoulder every step of the way.

'In a hurry?'

'Got to get my beauty sleep, you know.' She swiped the card. Red light. Swiped it again. Red. *Come on. Give me a break. Open up before I say or do something utterly stupid.*

'Need a hand?' He took the card from her fingers and swiped. 'There you go, first time lucky. If you need anything just holler. As luck would have it, I'm right next door.'

She swallowed hard. Closed the door behind him and breathed a silent goodnight. Then she switched the air conditioning to freeze-your-socks-off and prayed she could get through working in close proximity with Pretty Boy and the weird sensations rippling through her body. Glancing over to the interconnecting door she knew every ounce of her willpower would be tested to the limits.

CHAPTER THREE

As Zac stepped back for Dani to climb aboard the team coach ahead of him, excitement pinged through his veins, and not just because they were en route to the opening ceremony. If he thought seeing her in a cap and tracksuit would dampen his attraction to her he'd been sorely mistaken. He watched the tight curves under the figure-hugging black fabric and swallowed hard. To add insult to injury, the bus stank of muscle rub and testosterone, but the only thing filling his nostrils was jasmine and flowers.

As if his job wasn't hard enough.

For the past three hours they'd pummelled the players into some kind of shape. Worked smoothly side by side, focused and determined.

He hadn't been distracted by the soft texture of her skin, the way her eyes lit up when she smiled or the tiny mole just below her left eye. He hadn't thought about how good she'd felt in his arms as he'd escorted her into the ballroom last night. The way she raised his blood pressure—in a good way—even when she hurled abuse at him. In fact, he also hadn't lain awake thinking of her only feet away in the next room, wondering what she wore to bed. If anything. Nah, he hadn't thought about her at all.

Frustrating didn't come close. How the hell was he supposed to concentrate on making a good impression and getting the team match-fit if his head was constantly tuned to the bright light of her smile? Not to mention the sweet curve of her...

Focus.

He'd promised Tom he'd do this, chase his dream and make it work. As he thought about Tom again he fought against the memories that almost overwhelmed him—promises and guilt: a heady formula for success.

Now he surveyed the full coach with dismay. The only available seat was halfway down, next to her, and cheers erupted the length of the bus as he sat down next to her. He shook his head and wiggled towards the aisle. Too much closeness and too much Dani were stoking a heat in his groin that he needed to ignore. 'Looks like the Fates have put us together again.'

'Oh, lucky me.' She gave him a look that said she felt the opposite of lucky, but she winked in a kind of camaraderie way, long thick eyelashes grazing soft cheeks. Three hours of rubbing muscles and talking shoulder joint rehab had placed their relationship on a more even professional footing. Or so he wanted to believe.

He ignored the sarcasm and flicked his thumb behind them to the squad who were now singing the national anthem with great aplomb. 'At least someone's in good spirits.'

She shrugged, her cheeks pink, eyes gleaming, more with frustration than frivolity. 'You heard the boss, they should be focusing on the game plan, not getting carried away with the excitement.' She stood up and turned to the back of the bus. He had to admire her confidence. As a woman she seemed a little afraid of the world, but as a physio she oozed professionalism. Far from shouting, as he thought she'd do, she spoke to two players a few rows back in a quiet voice that commanded attention. Not the kind of leery attention she was probably used to—but sincere and genuine attention. She'd shown them in the treatment room that she could handle a hamstring strain as well as the next person. In the captain's run she'd managed the five kilometres as if it was a Sunday morning stroll and had worked through the injury list in a calm efficient manner. 'Okay, earphones in everyone. *Focus.* Jaxon, keep that thigh warm. Manu, if you stretch up like that again you'll end up being sidelined. Now settle down.'

Silence hit the bus like an out of control railroad truck. She sat and swiped her hands together. 'Well, that told them.'

'Sure did. Next time I need a bodyguard I'll know who to ask.'

That raised a brief smile, but her eyebrows lifted in derision. 'Don't you get carried away with the excitement as well, And don't forget I have a degree in doing odd things with sticky tape. And I'm not afraid to use it.'

So she wanted to play. He could play. One eye on the journey, the other on her. No harm done and a very nice way to get to the stadium. 'Sounds like fun. Any particular place on my body you'd prefer to start…?'

'Your too-smart mouth? And then…' Her eyes met his and heat zipped between them. The air around them palpably thickened and his gaze dropped to her lips. No lipstick today, but perfect pink lips pressed together in a sarcastic, possibly sadistic, smile. An unbidden need to run his tongue along those lips powered into his head.

No.

When he dragged his gaze back to her eyes he saw the hint of desire. God, he'd spent over a decade wooing women. He knew when a woman wanted him. And Dani's want fired something in him. It had been a long time since his body had reacted so strongly to a woman.

Then her father climbed aboard. And just like that her confidence seemed to leach out of her. She scanned Davide's every move as he waved royally to the players, then took the seat the driver had reserved for him up front. Her eyes fixed on the thick rolls of moley skin on the back of his neck; her hands fiddled with her hair as he'd seen her do twice already when she was nervous. Zac's hands clenched in an involuntary reaction—he knew how it felt to crave a father's attention, to be brought to the brink with anxiety. To be found wanting.

But whereas Zac had fought against it and thrown himself deep into proving himself in every which way he could, clearly Dani had internalised it all.

Once they'd set off Zac felt a tap on his shoulder and as he turned Matt thrust a tabloid newspaper in his hands. 'Here. Page twelve. Don't let her see it.'

'Oh, God.' A knot fisted in his gut as Zac twisted further into the aisle and peered at the grainy photograph of Dani and himself, arm in arm on the red carpet. The moment where he'd told her to imagine the hacks naked, her face alight with laughter looking up at him with bright eyes. The angle of the picture emphasised a closeness that hadn't been there.

The headline read *Lady Godiva and Sir Lancelot?*

Sir Love-A-Lot, more like. In a rare public outing celebrity recluse Dani Danatello and her rumoured-to-be new beau, Dr Zachary Price, walked the red carpet last night for a private charity ball organised by Danatello Investments. Clearly excited to be with him, Dani could barely keep her hands off her man, and who could blame her? Price has the allure and physique of one her father's rugby players. And a pedigree to match. His parents, Marguerite and Rufus Price, are the esteemed and outspoken heads of the internationally award-winning Price Institute of Geology. Famed for his denigration of popular culture and a society based on celebrity, excess and falling academic standards Rufus espoused his opinions in his recent book, Going to Hell. *So the* News Women's Page *can't help wondering what Rufus's reaction would be to his son mixing with the very type of people this leading academic scorns.*

'What's that?' Dani's voice got louder and the jasmine aroma intensified. The hairs on the back of Zac's neck prickled as he sensed her closing in. A sudden need to protect her mixed with the fury swimming in his gut, she didn't deserve such scrutiny and lies. And neither did he. If Davide got a whiff of this there'd be hell to pay.

Snapping the paper shut he forced a smile. 'Nothing. The usual dross.'

'You are such a bad liar. You do know that hiding it makes me want to read it even more? And I can buy it from the local store any time today. Or look it up on the internet.' She took out her phone and began jabbing at it.

'Okay, take it. But I'm warning you, it's not pretty.' He handed her the paper and shook his head. She was right—she'd see it anyway. Clearly she didn't want saving. She'd fought some demons and come out stronger, that was for sure. But that relentless attempt at jovial sarcasm was testament to a woman who didn't want to let anyone close. And yet, the message her eyes gave him, way too many times for him not to notice—the heat, the flash of reluctant desire—made him think she was fighting other demons too.

His heart thudded as she took the newspaper and scanned down. Her fine features hardened, her shoulders tightened. One small move and he could have had her in his arms, stroking her cheek, trying to protect her, but he controlled himself.

Protect her? Like he could. Like he'd be around long enough. Like he'd ever be fully available to give her what she needed.

The last time he'd been supposed to look out for someone he'd failed miserably. Hopelessly. And he'd been paying for it ever since. So this urge to protect Dani sounded warning bells. Already things were getting too personal. For God's sake, he hardly knew her.

But something inside her connected with something in him. That hadn't happened for a very long time.

He needed to shake it loose. Close off the feelings she stoked in him. Usually physical distance worked, but stuck on a bus in the only available seat made that impossible. He edged to the corner of the banquette. And watched her do the same. So the feeling was mutual. That suited him fine.

Outside, the crowds had thickened along the fan trail cheering the team bus along. Dotted along the route bands blasted out rousing tunes, stilt walkers and jugglers entertained the throngs. A flashmob dance troupe filled the road when the coach stopped at traffic lights. Flags with each team's colours adorned every pole and post. Outside the coach, the world had come to party. Inside, the silence hung around them like a weight pressing on his shoulders.

He scanned the players. Most of them had headphones on and seemed to be focusing on the beat. Occasionally one of them waved to the crowd. In a few minutes they'd be heading into what should be the most exciting thing to happen in his career to date and yet Zac's head whirred with a whole host of other emotions. One of which was anger. At himself. At the press. At Dani for instilling these kind of feelings in him. One minute he'd decided he should be far away from her, the next he wanted to hold her, protect her. He was mixed up and then some.

He kept his voice low as he pointed to the article. 'I'm sorry I caused all this. It definitely won't happen again.'

'And I'm sorry you've been embarrassed by your association with me.' She bristled. 'I'm sorry your parents will be horrified.'

He laughed ruefully. 'I'm thirty-four. It's been a long time since I cared what my parents think.' *Liar.*

'And yet when you say that you look away, as if you don't believe it yourself.' The light in her eyes, so clearly depicted in the photograph, had well and truly gone out.

'What will your father think?'

'Oh, yes. Of course, the most important issue for us all. Never mind how to deal with the gross invasion of privacy, conjecture and outright lies, but what will Davide think? He'll be furious, probably because he hadn't thought of it himself.' Now the light was replaced with the kind of scorn equal only to his own father's. The barriers he'd glimpsed last night were well and truly locked in place. Her head shook and she bit the corner of her lip. 'But it'll get you noticed. Which, I guess, is what you wanted all along.'

She thought he wanted Davide's approval? Well, didn't he? 'I was honestly trying to help you. I didn't do it to get Davide's attention. I'm not like that. Why would you think that?'

'Because, in my experience, that's what people do. You're in his management team, aren't you? Surely it must have crossed your mind that if you do well here you'll have endless offers…perhaps the national team? Doesn't every New Zealand sports doctor want to work with the All Blacks?'

He couldn't deny it was top of his wish-list. 'Well…'

'Ching. Ching. Out of time, Dr Price. Your pause says it all. You're one of those alpha types who have to succeed, and being associated with me won't hurt. Right? Hoping I might put a good word in? Using me to get to my dad?'

'You're twisting things.'

'No, honey, *you* twisted it last night when you took my arm in front of the paparazzi.' She looked like she wanted to twist some other part of him. He crossed his legs.

'I was trying to rescue you.'

'When will you get it into that thick skull of yours? I don't need rescuing.' Her fist wrapped round a chunk of hair, then she pressed it against her mouth. But this time he let her go right on and do it, guessing another overt gesture of helpfulness wouldn't go down too well right now.

He pointed to the picture of their so-called public display of affection. They looked damned good together, that he couldn't deny. 'Oh, come on. It's not that bad. It could have been worse, at least they got my good side.'

'Do you have one?' She glared at him. 'Is this all just a joke to you?'

Far from it.

The bus pulled up at the stadium, fans clustered into the car park and loud cheers resonated across the skies. Zac raised his voice slightly, but not loud enough that anyone else would hear. 'I'm trying to maintain a sense of humour and not ruin what's going to be a great day.' He smiled, trying to convince her. 'Besides, that journalist needs to check her facts. She's got the two stories mixed up. Lady Godiva had absolutely nothing to do with Sir Lancelot. They certainly weren't in any kind of relationship.'

Dani gathered up her bags, stood and pierced him with a look of disdain that left nothing to his imagination. 'And that's exactly how it's going to stay.'

They were losing.

Didn't matter that she'd done her job to perfection. Had stuck to the game plan, managed the sideline checks, seamlessly relayed information to the coach via wireless headset microphone. Didn't matter how consummate a professional she looked, how dedicated or competent. Didn't matter because once the players were on the pitch it was out of her control.

At half time she'd brought Jaxon back from a close injury call and iced three hamstrings and a shoulder. Stuck them back together again.

They needed to score. And fast.

Zac sat next to her on the bench, his right leg jigging up and down to some beat only he could hear. 'Ten minutes to go. We need to pull something out of the bag or we'll go into the next game on the back foot. We have to beat this lot—they're the weakest team in the pool.'

'And losing the first game will make them the laughing-stock of the tournament.' Just another thing to add to her father's mounting ire. If he saw the photograph in the paper his anger would fire off the scale, meaning she'd have to try even harder to make him happy.

And just to add to the tension she had the biggest crush of her life on the one person she needed to stay well away from.

Despite the trouble he'd caused, her body had decided it quite liked Zachary Price and was on an all-out bid to convince her brain. Every time she set eyes on him her skin tingled—unless he broke her out in hives which, seeing how irritating he was, could be eminently feasible. But she got hot in places that had never been hot before. Her heart did a funny arrhythmic dance.

This never happened. Never could happen. Not when her focus was on her father. Which was why she needed to adopt all-out avoidance tactics. Not easy when she was stuck with Zac almost 24/7.

She scanned the pitch for any playing concerns.

Jaxon motioned from the field; his thigh injury was obviously causing him distress. 'Hey, Coach.' She clicked the switch and spoke into the mic. 'Next time there's a break in play we'll have to sort out Jaxon's hamstring. I'd suggest bringing him off, but we need him.'

'Got you.' Matt's disjointed voice crackled down.

'Come on, Jets.' Zac yelled, and shifted in his seat. His smell wafted around her. She forced back the million things his proximity made her want to do. Hit him. Hold him. Kiss him.

And then suddenly he was running onto the pitch screaming at her to bring the bag, the ice. Her arrhythmia kicked into full force as she grabbed at the equipment and raced towards the player prone on the grass.

'Manu? Manu? Can you hear me?' Zac tapped the player's cheek. 'Manu?'

'Yeah?' Manu's voice sounded fractured and hazy.

Zac tipped his head up and looked at her, his eyes cautious but determined. 'Hey, Dani. Head collision. The other one's okay. Their doctor's seeing to him.'

'You want to bring him off?'

'Let's see if he can stand.' He shifted an arm under Manu's back and manoeuvred him upright. The player staggered to the left but Zac held on to his arm. 'You okay, mate?'

'Yeah. Gotta stay and play, though.'

Dani smiled and inched closer to him, aware that this game was possibly the most important in Manu's life. He wouldn't want to come off, however badly hurt he was, so they needed to deal with this delicately. A concerned hum rippled round the stadium at one of the star players being injured in the first game. The TV cameras would be fixed on them. She tried to concentrate on their patient, not on the large screens showing her in close-up or on Zac. Definitely not on Zac. 'Manu. There's only a few minutes left to go. Let's get that head looked at so you can play next round.'

'I'm good. I can stay on.'

'No, mate. I'm telling you. You're coming off.' She flicked her switch again. 'Bringing him off, Matt.'

'Says who?' Manu's manner darkened. He jumped up and lurched forward, his large face inches from hers, blood running down his cheek from a gash on his forehead, his teeth bared. His eyes looked like they were trying to focus, with little success. If she'd met him in a dark alleyway she'd have run in the opposite direction. Right now she had to face him down in front of the crowd. 'You're not the coach. You're just a woman. What do you know? I'm staying. Okay?'

'Enough.' Zac stood between them and faced off the six-feet-two player. Determined, but assertive, Zac's voice held no nonsense and just enough empathy. 'Listen. You need a thorough assessment. Head injuries can be a lot worse than just a headache and blurred vision. I'm not taking any risks. As for Dani? She's our physio, so you'll listen to her. And I'm the doctor, and right now we're in charge. We're both telling you, you need to get off the pitch. Now.' Then he looped his arm round the player's shoulder and frog marched him to the sideline.

The raging tachycardia didn't stop until she left the field accompanied by a round of applause. Although she knew that was probably for Manu's efforts earlier in the game rather than anything the medical team had done.

'Is he okay?' she asked Zac, who was handing their patient over to the ambulance service pitch-side. He flicked his phone into his pocket.

'Mild concussion, I imagine. Hence the volatile temper. He'll be fine. I've just organised an assessment by a neurologist—they're taking him now.'

'Good.' Although she could have dealt with Manu on her own she'd been glad for Zac's support. He'd taken a candid attitude in a situation that needed to be dealt with quickly.

Even though she was loath to admit, Zac had so far proved to be a skilled doctor and negotiator.

She couldn't help but steal just another quick glimpse of his face. The tiny dimple that winked at her with every smile. The deep warmth in those dark brown eyes. The strength in the arms that had almost carried a grown man off the pitch. She knew how it felt to be wrapped in them and had a wicked ache to be there again.

A roar reverberated around the crowd. No. She'd missed something important. She turned quickly to watch the replay on the large TV screen.

A try! A try by the Jets, nudging them into a draw. One swift conversion kick and they'd be in the lead. Along with the rest of the crowd she held her breath as Jaxon stepped up to kick. She had to hand it to him; he always seemed so self-assured. Like Zac. That God-given confidence that some men had in abundance. That Zac wore like a comfortable suit.

The ball flew over the bar. The final whistle blew. Game over. They'd won. One hurdle down, another two hundred to go.

She blew out a breath and forced more air back into her lungs. Her father would be pleased. That would make her existence happier until the next game in a few days. No major injuries, excepting a head injury.

She just had to remember to concentrate on the game and not on that alluring dimple.

'You okay, Daniella?' Zac caught her up along the player's tunnel en route to the treatment room. The way he said her name made her stomach flip. No one ever called her that unless she was in serious trouble, but he made it sound pretty. Sexy. It had been a very long time since she'd felt sexy. So she was definitely in trouble. 'I see a lot of icing and strapping in your future.'

Concentrate on work. 'Yes, but nothing too major, apart from Manu. They'll all live.'

He touched her arm, stopped her in her tracks and waited until the tunnel had emptied. 'Are *you* okay?'

'Sure. Why?' The way he looked at her with such concern was disconcerting. Did he think she was weak? 'You think I can't handle this?'

'Absolutely you can. I've no doubt at all.' His hand reached out towards her cheek for a split second, then he appeared to have second thoughts. 'You looked a bit shaken when Manu lunged at you. I was worried.'

'Whoa? Pretty Boy turning soft?' *Please don't do this. Don't be nice. Nice is too difficult to resist.* 'I could have handled it. I'm not a helpless cavewoman, even though you act like a Neanderthal.'

'I can't help it.' He grinned, leaned over and whispered close to her ear. Once again his hot breath tickled her skin. Heat pooled in her abdomen, then rippled out in wave after wave of disturbing but delicious sensations through her body. 'You bring out the caveman in me, all restless and fighting and needing to protect.'

'Well, go and protect someone else. Somewhere else. I hear there are a lot of damsels in distress in Siberia. Mongolia?' Anywhere but in this deserted dark tunnel. 'We've got to go and run the injury clinic. The last thing I need is more ill-informed gossip.'

'We could give them something to gossip about.' His lips curled into a tantalising smile. He watched her reaction, seemingly mesmerised by the emotions she knew were crossing her face. So much for avoidance tactics. No matter how hard she tried to remain impartial about him, she failed.

His smile reached dark brown eyes that promised her a million sins. 'I've been thinking about that sex ban. I'm compiling a list of all the things we could do that don't involve the actual act. More like *sex-free* sex. Everything…but.'

Now his hand touched her shoulder, firing intense shivers of heat into her stomach. His voice, deeper, edgier. 'So how about you help me come up with a few ideas? I vote for…stroking first. Lots and lots of stroking.'

'Zac.' She tried for a warning tone, but it came out more like a squeak. A breathless, wanton squeak.

'Hmm? Here. And here. Stroking. Touching. *Rubbing.*' His fingers walked slowly from her shoulder, to her neck. To that sensitive dip above her collarbone. She curled instinctively into his touch. The fantasy and the danger threatening to send her over the edge. Before she knew it she'd be adding to that list.

No—she'd be writing her own. How did it go? Hit him…? 'And now you're a walking, talking thesaurus?'

'But you like it. I can tell.'

She shook her head and closed her eyes. Take control.

Five. Four. Three. Two. One. But counting backwards from three thousand probably wouldn't be enough. She purposefully loaded her prosaic schoolmarm voice that she used with the unruly kids at work. 'How about emigration? Castration?'

'You're getting the hang of it, but it needs work.'

At the smirk on his face she hardened. 'Look, Zachary. I told you before…I'm just not interested.'

'So say it like you mean it and I'll walk.…'

'Ahem. Now, now, children. Play nicely.' Matt's voice crackled loudly into Dani's ear. 'Can you two kiss and make up quickly, then get down here. Davide's demanding to talk to you both about that newspaper photo. And I'm up to my neck in sticking plaster.'

CHAPTER FOUR

'WHAT?' ZAC GLARED right back at the coach across the small treatment room. The interminable debrief was thankfully coming to an end and he would finally be able to get his head together. Impossible to do when the place was wall-to-wall with management suits and freshly laundered players. And only if he could get Matt off his case. He looked like he had a bad case of terminal indigestion—all bloated and blotchy faced. With Davide's back turned the coach chopped his fingers across his throat. *Stop.* Zac interpreted. *Cut it out.*

So what? He was a highly skilled professional, not some unruly hormone-crazed teenager. And he'd speak with Dani any way he liked. Even if it did mean out-of-bounds top-notch flirting. Because, well, she was good at it, and stopping would be such a waste. It wasn't doing anyone any harm.

Next time he'd make sure her earpiece was turned off.

Next time... Okay. Sense flooded back with the blood to his brain. There shouldn't be a next time.

His head pounded. He'd so nearly kissed her. Temptation had pulled him closer to those divine lips, the smile hovering over her mouth attracting him like a bee to a honeypot. And God, yes, he'd been rattled by Manu's attack on her. Some feral force inside him had made him want to protect her, and flatten Manu.

His track record in protection didn't exactly shine with excellence. So right now he needed to stop with this insane urge to save her and focus more on saving his job.

Danatello turned and surveyed the group. His steely glare fixed each person in turn.

'Not good enough, team. A narrow victory clawed from the jaws of defeat. We have to do better.' Zac understood how the man had become so successful; he dominated the room, his voice like clear cut crystal.

Like Zac's own father Davide could wither people with a stare and failure wasn't an option. But unlike Zac's dusty, stuffy father with his padded elbows and baggy khakis, Davide had Mr Business written all over him. And with fat ruddy cheeks, rotund belly and periodic sharp intakes of breath he was a high-fat, high-stress heart attack waiting to happen. Although Zac doubted the boss would ever let him close enough with a stethoscope to check him out. 'We need more pressure up front. Early attack. *More focus*. We'll talk more tomorrow. Bed now, everyone. Apart from the doc and Dani, I need a quick word with you both.'

Beside him, Zac felt Dani's breathing increase and her body tense. His senses firing on full alert whenever he was near her was becoming a habit. The blood rushed from his brain back to his groin. Which seemed, so far, to activate his flirt mechanism and left little room for making good decisions.

Out of the corner of his eye he saw her telltale finger-wrapped-round-with-hair habit. Any second now it would reach her mouth. He waited.

Bingo. Her teeth nibbled around her finger...her eyes hooded and cautious. And it hit him then that standing in front of Davide wasn't just a minor irritation for Dani, it was full-blown stress. Gone was the competent physiotherapist who'd looked Manu in the eye and told him she was boss. And back now was the cautious girl he'd glimpsed last night on the red carpet. The one who tried to show the world she could handle anything. But this? This softening made his heart ache.

If this was the kind of anxious reaction she had in Davide's presence, then Zac vowed to put her under no further pressure with flirty games. This wasn't an easy score, or a quick wrestle between the sheets. This was a woman who clearly craved her father's approval. And he wouldn't be the one to snatch that away from her.

As the last person left the room he took control. 'Mr Danatello, the story in the papers is pure fabrication. Just a whole load of sensational nonsense.'

'So there's nothing I should know?' Davide pierced Zac with an unwavering stare as he threw a newspaper onto the table. His finger jabbed at the grainy photograph. 'I hate surprises. I hate being lied to. I hate being kept in the dark about anything. And I mean...anything.'

Although he'd seen scant evidence of it in his own life Zac understood a father's need to protect. But something about Danatello made him think the entrepreneur had a different agenda—not so much protecting his daughter, more power and control.

'My private life's not open to scrutiny, Davide. But, for the record, Dani and I met for the first time on the red carpet and we walked into the dinner together. That's it. The photograph was taken from an odd angle. No further discussion needed. There's nothing more between us.' Yeah, right. Like the more he said it, the more it'd be true?

'No, Daddy. There is absolutely nothing going on.' Again he felt Dani stiffen beside him, her voice wavering. 'I'm sorry about all this fuss.'

Zac turned and saw her crestfallen face, her slumped shoulders. Shoot, this was the twenty-first century—no woman should feel under that kind of pressure to make a man happy. Especially when it was Zac's fault, not hers. His hands fisted at his sides. All his life he'd wished he'd stood up to his own father, now he could at least do it for Dani.

'I took Dani's arm to steer her through the barrage of intrusive journalists. I'm not sorry at all and I'd do it again in a flash. But I am disappointed a man and woman can't be seen together in public without gossip and innuendo. And that people actually care about the rubbish they read.' He glared at Danatello, hoping his message would get across. *Back off.* With his job on the line he had to pick his words carefully. Ignoring Danatello's open mouth he fixed his gaze on Dani. 'We work well together and we'll make a good team. I only care about helping the Jets win. That's all. I'll see you in the morning.'

Dani caught up with Zac in the foyer waiting for the lift. Would every evening end with them zooming skywards with no words and a raging tension between them? *Bring on the final and then home, sweet home.*

But instead of dampening her irrational attraction to him the whole scenario had heightened it. The guy had *powerful* honed to perfection. He turned and fixed her with an intense gaze filled with passion and strength, and the force of it hit her hard in the solar plexus. Gone was the playboy flirt, here was a man of substance. In fact, everything she'd seen of him today—in the treatment room, pitch-side, with her father, had fitted pieces to a jigsaw that made him gloriously whole. Professional, charismatic. Desirable. Sex on legs. Very nice legs, very muscly legs, if the outline of his trousers was anything to go by.

He managed a smile, his shoulders relaxing in his smart designer suit as the light filtered back into his eyes. Warm honey flecked those pools of deep brown and heat fizzed in her abdomen.

What was happening to her? This wasn't sensible Dani who worked hard to keep everything under control.

Something inside was struggling to break free—her long-repressed sense of fun, perhaps? Devil-may-care? But look where that had got her before... And she wasn't headed that way again any time soon.

Being caught out having a sexy conversation, like a naughty schoolgirl, had ignited a playful part of her that had been dormant for too long. It had been years since she'd felt so frivolous and alive.

But the only things that mattered were winning the tournament, getting back on track with Daddy and making amends for the past. Zac was in the way. A roadblock that she needed to steer round. One that, right now, shook with anger. So she needed to try to smooth over their working relationship. 'Thanks for what you said in there, Zac. At least we're all clear.'

'Absolutely crystal.' He shook his head. 'Your father's really something.'

'He is. Don't worry, you won't lose your job. He's hot-headed and volatile but not stupid. Where would he get a replacement doctor in the middle of a tournament?'

'He doesn't have a spare doctor daughter lurking in the shadows?'

'Not that I know of.' She laughed.

For all his faults Davide was still her father and that fierce love she had for him failed to diminish no matter how much he pushed her away. At least he hadn't suggested the tabloid photos had been a good thing, and set them up with some sort of media-frenzied magazine shoot like Deanna. And at least Zac hadn't sold her out, like Paul had. Yet. It was early days and there was still time for him to show his true colours. Where men like her father were concerned it seemed there were no depths to which they'd stoop. Unfortunately, it was always to her cost.

'I get the feeling he wouldn't care about sacking anyone if they got on his wrong side.' Zac pounded the lift button with his fist. 'Does he even have a right side?'

'Oh, yes.' *I just haven't found it yet.* But she would, before it was too late. She forced a smile. 'Ever since my mother died he's struggled to keep a lid on his temper. She was his mellow voice of reason.'

Zac swivelled to face her, his manner softening, anger turned to sadness in those dark brown eyes. 'I'm sorry.'

'Don't be. It was a long, long time ago. I barely remember her.' *And don't pity me.*

'So you put up with him acting like that even now?'

She lifted her chin and plastered on her plastic smile. Because it was too complicated to share things about her relationship with her family. 'Yes. Yes, we do. You wouldn't understand.'

His arm leaned lazily against the elevator frame. 'Try me.'

'No. I don't want to try anything with you, Zac.

He leaned closer. 'Liar.'

God, yes. But she wasn't going to act on it. 'Not even tempted.'

He stepped closer. 'No? You sure?'

'Positively.'

'That's not what your eyes are telling me. Your eyes tell me lots of things, Dani. What you're thinking...what you want. How you feel.'

No way. She hadn't spent years building barriers just for him to blast them away. 'Well, let these words tell you exactly how I feel, Zachary. Butt out.' She snapped her eyes closed and breathed out. Hard.

After a few moments she took a chance, opened one eye to find him staring at the elevator door. She watched his face, the upturned corners of his delicious mouth, travelled lower to the hard wall of chest, the way his trousers curved around a perfectly formed butt.

And then reactivated her avoidance plan.

Dodging past him into the lift she pressed the eleventh-floor button, but he jumped in next to her. A thousand questions ran across his gaze and she turned away unable to give him any answers. The oppressive heat of the late-summer evening pressed against her, that and the unbearable harsh thump of her heart made her struggle to catch her breath.

For long seconds she was aware of nothing but the beat of her heart, the slam of desire in her chest. The agony of wanting him and knowing it could never happen, and the ecstasy of being held in the heat of those eyes. However many times she told herself to keep away from him, he drew her closer, like a magnetic force tugging her north.

A quick jerk and the lift started its ascent. Her stomach flipped and her heart danced. Despite all her resolve she couldn't pretend she didn't want to touch him. He may have been way off limits but, damn, he was beautiful.

His white dress shirt looked so starched and new she wondered how much his heat had softened it. Just one fingertip running along that line of tiny pearl buttons would tell her. His hands, gripping the rail, looked capable and strong. She imagined what pleasure they could give her. A low hum started in her abdomen, stroked her deep inside.

Memories of last night, his touch on her arm, jumbled into her head. His scent washed over her, that same exotic spice, making her feel dizzy. How would his lips taste? How would he take her? Sweet and slow or hard and fast? She knew he wanted her. Had known since the second he'd looked at her on that red carpet, the sharp flash of awareness fired in his eyes. And it hadn't dimmed. If anything it blazed more brightly.

Oblivious to the carnal thoughts zipping round her head he lounged casually against the handrail, his image multiplied a thousand times in the large mirrors. Everywhere she looked he filled her vision. Even when she closed her eyes.

Was it a weakness to wish the lift would break down? Right now. Right when they were alone. To turn to him in the dark and press her lips against his. To taste him, to feel his body against hers. In here, where no one would ever know. Where there were no cameras. Where her father's stupid celibacy rules couldn't matter. Where she could take a risk and do something rash and fun without worrying about the consequences or broken trust.

To halt time…just for a few seconds.

She opened her eyes and focused on the big red emergency stop button. *Please stop. Stop.*

Suddenly, as if answering her prayers, the lights flickered and the lift jolted.

There was a God!

Grabbing on to his arm to steady herself—and just for the sheer delight of touching him—she laughed. Then the lift pinged at level eleven and the doors whooshed open.

Maybe there wasn't a God after all. Or maybe some annoyingly chaste goody-two-shoes was just looking out for her. *Gee, thanks, buster.*

She blew out a deep sigh. Just for a moment she'd dared to dream, but the idea of kissing him lodged centre stage in her brain. Letting go of his arm was impossible, her legs wouldn't take her weight and if she did let go she'd crumple in a heap at his feet. So not the sophisticated image she wanted to portray. So she hung on to the dark navy sleeve.

'Come on, princess, time for bed. It's been a long day.' He pressed his palm over her hand so tenderly she wanted to cry. How could he do *nice* when she wanted him to do *down and dirty*? But the tenderness struck a chord—the man was definitely the whole package. Or he certainly played the whole package...and she was falling for it, hook, line and sinker.

Well, she wouldn't. The last thing she needed was to lose her heart to another charmer who'd use her as a stepping stone to his own success.

Trying hard not to inhale his smell or relish the heat emanating from his body that in turn stoked a fire in her belly, she brushed past him into the empty landing.

Somehow his arms folded round her. 'Dani?'

'Yes?' She found her voice, but it was cracked and hoarse, thick with desire. His face was a heartbeat from hers; the soft breeze of his breath caressed her skin.

She wouldn't lose her heart to him. Would not. She could protect herself well; she had enough willpower and self-control to keep from ever being vulnerable again.

But, hell, she wanted him. An innate physical ache. Her heart did the macarena as she palmed his chest, stepped her fingers down his shirt. Hot body. Soft shirt. Hard... 'Is there something you want, Zac?'

'I keep telling myself no. But...damn it. Yes.' His eyes held just one question now and she still didn't know the answer, didn't know what was right or wrong, up or down, didn't know anything except that the ache to seal her lips against his wouldn't leave her.

Nice morphed into naughty. With one swift move he flicked her baseball cap off her head, then shook her curls loose and tangled his fingers in her hair. At the gentle touch of his hands she closed her eyes, her body pulsing with a raging need that both startled and threatened to overwhelm her. Her self-control pooled into nothing...Zac was too much to refuse. This was too much to refuse.

He paused, his mouth inches away from hers. The tiny pulse at the base of his neck beat wildly, his breathing ragged. Tension and anger and desire rebounded off him and fuelled her need for him. 'About that list.'

'The sex-free sex list?'

'Yes. I'm adding to it all the time.' His tongue traced a tender path along her bottom lip. 'Kissing?'

'Aha.'

'Sucking.' He sucked her lip into his mouth, then nipped it gently between his teeth. Let it go and smiled. 'Biting.'

'*God*. Yes.'

Then his lips were on hers. Gentle at first, a tender pressure that deepened as she opened her mouth to him. The first touch of his tongue sent electricity zinging through her veins. His hands circled her waist and pulled her closer, his arousal evident in the hardness pressing against her belly. She opened her eyes, reached up on her tiptoes and watched the look of exquisite joy on his face as she deepened the kiss. He tasted just like she knew he would, of man and sex and something exquisite. A deep groan erupted from his throat, sending shock waves of want spiralling through her body.

Eventually she ripped her mouth away, inhaled deeply to steady herself. Looked up into those dark eyes that stole her breath. 'Well, wow, Dr Price. Not half bad. Is this the way you say goodnight to all your colleagues?'

'Nah, I heard Matt's a rubbish kisser. You, however...' He leaned back in for round two. 'And I thought you weren't even tempted? Tut tut,' he murmured into her mouth, then his lips traced a trail of kisses down her neck. 'So much for me being on my best behaviour. You're leading me astray.'

She curled into his heat. 'It's a temporary lapse. I'll be right back to normal.... Oooh, this is heaven.' This was intoxicating. Addictive.

This was... A red light up in the corner of the ceiling

distracted her. A smoke alarm? A CCTV camera? Anger mixed with the fire surging through her. Would she ever be allowed some privacy?

This was way past stupid.

She pushed her palms against his chest and stepped back, swiped her hand against swollen lips. 'I've got to go.'

'Hey. What does that mean?'

She waited for him to call her a tease, but he just stared at her, confusion and the dying traces of desire in his eyes.

It means I'm losing my marbles. 'It means I'm going to bed. It means this shouldn't have happened and it won't ever happen again. Think of your job. Of Davide.'

She stumbled to her hotel room door, all the while feeling the glare of his disappointed gaze on her back. The fading heat of the kiss, the fun of doing something dangerous and unpredictable, fizzled into the dry stale air. This time the swipe card worked like a dream. But once again she leaned back against the door and pressed her fingertips around her temples trying to calm down, to rid herself of the intense hum zipping through her body.

'Three hundred. Two hundred and ninety-nine. Two hundred and ninety-bloody-eight...'

After two rounds she was back in control.

She stalked to the bathroom and shoved a glass under the cold water tap, ran the rim over her forehead. 'Go to hell with your stupid list, and leave me alone.'

She stared at her reflection in the mirror, at her dishevelled hair and bruised lips, so unused to kissing. The telltale misty eyes that told her she'd been on a hiding to nothing. No way would she allow a man to disrupt the life she'd made for herself. No way would she fall under the spell of yet another gold-digger, or plain outright liar.

The kiss had been a minor slip. Straightening her shoulders as she scrubbed make-up remover over her cheeks she talked sense to herself. 'Daniella Danatello, you are a good person. You have not failed. One smoking-hot kiss does not mean you have no self-control.'

One smoking-hot kiss would not change the fact that men were off limits.

One smoking-hot kiss did not break her father's celibacy rule.

One smoking-hot kiss... But damn, it had been good.

CHAPTER FIVE

'So, spill the goss. What's Dr Delicious like to work with? Soooo cute.' Desere sighed, and checked herself in the gaudy gilt-edged hotel bathroom mirror as she applied the glossiest red lipstick Dani had ever seen.

Dani deflected the conversation away from Zac. With a bit of luck Desere wouldn't notice. 'Nice lippy. Suits you.'

'Gorgeous, isn't it? Freebie from Fashion Week.' Her sister waved the lipstick in front of Dani's face. All thoughts of previous conversations clearly evaporated at the mention of make-up. 'Only twenty in the whole country and the waiting list is huge. You should put your name down.'

'Hmm. I can wait.'

Desere smoothed down her two-sizes-too-small tee and checked her sprayed-on snakeskin jeans-clad backside from all angles. 'Ohmygod, this lighting is a disaster. I look terrible.'

Dani tried to mould her frown into a saintly smile. But failed, badly. Why did everything have to revolve around how her sister looked and not what she did? But then what did Desere do, apart from smile and preen in designer dresses and do her father's bidding? Desere made vacuous an art form. Thankfully. At least now Zac was lost somewhere in the empty corners of her sister's brain. 'Deanna, you look amazing. As always.'

'And you could too. If only you'd make an effort. Look at that tracksuit. So shapeless.' She unzipped Dani's top to expose a bit of cleavage. 'Doesn't show off your best assets. Next year we'll get Luigi to design the team outfit—he'd know how to work it for you. Now, we need to get going.'

'I don't need assets when I'm working and I need to be comfortable on a team-bonding trip…wait…' Dani zipped her top up to her chin, then held up her finger. '*We* need to get going?' Reality seeped into her muddled head. Thinking straight since Zac's kiss two days ago had been almost impossible. For some reason every time she found herself next to him in the treatment room she wanted to add things to his stupid list. 'Firstly, wives and girlfriends are supposed to be banned from the hotel. And secondly, you're dressed… *down*. You didn't just drop by to say hello to me, did you? You're coming with us? On the helicopter sky tour and the jet-boat ride?' She struggled to control the irritation. Typical Desere to muscle in on the perks of the job. When would she stop interfering in her life?

'Daddy wanted all his girls here to up the *wow* factor for the media coverage. It's our last chance before you go into closed camp in Rotorua tomorrow. So, I guess you could say I'm working too.' She smiled the famous Desere Danatello smile, slightly tilted jaw, perfect teeth and come-to-bed eyes. The spontaneous look she'd spent years perfecting. 'We can't all indulge ourselves with a little *profession*. Some of us need to uphold the family reputation.'

Desere tapped Dani on the nose as if she were her pesky chihuahua. And for a moment, Dani imagined how wonderful it would be to run off back to her cosy anonymous cottage, and leave them all to it. Her sisters, father, the whole charade. But leaving them without a physio would only bring more shame on the Danatello name—like she hadn't made a profession out of that already.

Her big sister scrutinised her. 'Okay, let me wield some magic. Just a little hitch of the strap here. A stray lock of hair here. A smudge of lip gloss. Pinked-up cheeks.'

'Desere, I can manage quite well on my own.'

'Never turn down an offer of help from an expert, darling.' Dani had given up trying to stop her doing this. She sucked in the nightmare—as soon as Desere was gone she'd wipe the mess off. Easier to do that than to have her sister sulking. Desere stepped back to admire her handiwork. 'Pretty. And I don't think I'm the only one to think so.'

Dani's heart hammered against her rib cage. 'Oh?'

'Oh? Dr Delicious, oh? Dr you're-just-too-good-to-be-true. Dr can't-take-my-eyes-off-you.' And now the nightmare came with a cheesy soundtrack. 'Come on, Dani, the man's hot for you.'

'Don't be ridiculous.'

'Strange, I know, when you spend the day wearing shapeless tracksuits. But hey, who am I to judge?'

'Because that's what you do best.' What the whole Danatello clan did. Poor? Don't bother speaking to us. Unimportant? Average? Get in line.

Years ago Dani had longed for a regular sister she could confide in. To talk about things like the earth-shattering kiss. About the confusion Zac had wreaked in her body and her head. To ask what to do. What to say. How to feel. But Desere surely wasn't the right person. Had never been. Since the death of their mother Desere had moulded herself into being Daddy's right-hand woman.

In the end Dani had learned it was easier to keep her own counsel—or share with her friends, the people she could truly trust, back home in Wellington. Far away from this madness. 'Zac's just a colleague.'

'Don't frown, darling. You'll get premature lines. Maybe you should start with some fillers soon?' Desere blotted her lips on a tissue from the jewel-encrusted tissue box. Stacked high with cologne, deodorant, fluffy startlingly white face cloths, the executive suite bathroom lacked nothing. 'Colleague or not. The man's a god.'

A god with a dirty mind. And hot hands. And a list... Dani bit the inside of her cheek and held back the smile. 'Haven't noticed.'

'Then you need your eyes tested. Okay. Let's go.' Picking up her clutch her sister opened the bathroom door.

But she wouldn't let the Zac subject drop.

In the hallway. ''Do you know how highly Daddy rates him? Word is, as soon as this tournament's over the doc's jumping ship.'

This was news. 'Oh? To where?'

'Bigger and better. National teams? Olympic committee?'

Dani shouldn't have been surprised. He was good at what he did. At *everything* he did. Seduction. Kissing...

In the lift. 'He'd be a great asset if he were to stay here permanently. If you know what I mean.' She winked.

Getting tired of the innuendo Dani went for plain talking. 'Let's get this straight. You want me to ask him to stay on? Like what I say to him will make a difference? I'm sure Zac will do whatever he wants to without me interfering.'

'I'm not asking you to interfere. But there are other things you could do to make it more...attractive for him to stay.'

Was this for real? Desere honestly thought it would be that easy to entice a man into signing a contract? But then, heck, she'd done it with Joseph. But what about the life Dani had so carefully created for herself? In Wellington? Far away from the Auckland Jets. 'You want me to seduce him? Does Daddy know? What about his rules?'

'Since when did you ever follow Daddy's rules, sweetie?'

'Ouch.' But sure, she had a point. And Dani had set her heart on finding favour with Davide again. But not like this. There was a limit to how far she was willing to take this thing she had for Zac. And it ended with that kiss. 'No way. No way.'

In the lobby. 'I'm just saying, you could *encourage* him to stay after the tournament. It wouldn't be such a hardship. Just look at him.'

Dani followed her sister's gaze to the huddle of men waiting for them in the middle of the hotel lobby. Without intending to, without seeking him out, he was the first man her eyes settled on. As broad and tall as the players any other man might have faded into the mass of testosterone and sharp shaven jaws. But Zac stood out, radiating charisma and confidence. His smile, as always, turning her steady heart rate to a jumping mess. Damn him.

Desere's voice lowered as she wrapped Dani into a hug. 'Think about it, sis. It's not all about you. It's about family. Family's what's important. Keep the doctor here. What is it they say? Take one for the team. Do it for Daddy.'

Love her or hate her, and Dani regularly veered between the two, Desere knew exactly where to stick the knife. Dani rose above her sister's stupid idea, looked beyond her and over to Zac. If anything happened between them it would be pure and based on honesty.

'No, Des. Not happening. I'm not prostituting myself for anyone. Ever. Paul's fake proposal was bad enough.' There'd been too much pretence in her love life already. She'd never do that willingly. Even if it meant the rift between herself and Davide never healed.

But now wasn't the time or the place to further this conversation. There were cameras. And even though on the red carpet she'd let them get to her, she was never going to allow that again. She jutted her chin, sucked in her stomach and breathed in. This time she would show them.

'Give them your best smile, Daniella. And think about

it. Catching a man for Daddy would be easy payback.' Desere pulled away slightly. A frown line she would have been mortified to know about appeared on her forehead; the light in her green eyes dulled a little. For the first time ever, Dani glimpsed a flicker of weariness. 'It's not so bad. Honestly.'

So plan A hadn't quite panned out the way Zac had imagined. The whole *colleagues* thing had morphed suddenly into way more than that. Crazy didn't describe it. One minute he'd vowed not to flirt. The next he'd had her in his arms.

It had taken hours to slow his tachycardia, to deal with the excess adrenalin surging round his body. And he'd given up trying to extinguish the image of her face from his brain; it was getting close to a point where he couldn't think straight. There was a duel raging between his head and his heart.

Which was why he needed to have that conversation with her. The one that went, *Great kiss, but...*

Before he got in any deeper.

Trouble was, she'd perfected the art of avoidance. Or tried to wither him with a stare any time he got too close.

And now with Davide and Matt at some important coaches' meeting, he and Dani were playing minders to a bunch of hyped-up athletes.

Having been assigned the last helicopter he was running late but caught up with her at the front of the jet-boat queue trying to keep twenty-two men under control.

She nodded towards him but her manner was as cold as the ocean. 'Joseph, get back here, the boat's leaving in a minute. Manu, put the ball away. It'll end up in the water and you with it.'

Zac shook his head. Since she only responded to anything rugby-related at the moment he went for that. 'Don't worry, princess, they'll quieten down once they're on the boat. Nothing like a thick metal seatbelt to inflict restraint.'

She fixed him with that stare again. 'Sorry. You talking to me?'

'Don't see anyone else who might fit that description. Apart from possibly our new superstar game maker turned diva, Jaxon. Or your lovely sister.' He nodded over to where Desere stood in the shade in the highest heels and tightest jeans he'd ever seen. Whoever christened her as demure needed their eyes tested. And as for dazzling Deanna... Dani beat them in both stakes, hands down.

Desere waved her middle three fingers and winked. At him? No. At Dani. Strange. But that was sisters for you. 'She just winked.'

'Ignore her. She'll be going soon. For a start she'll never get on the boat in those shoes, and secondly, the wind and the spray will ruin her hair and she'd never let that happen. She's only here for the photos. But I'm sure she'd love to talk to you. She's a big fan. Apparently. Go ahead. Meanwhile I'll attempt to do our job and control the mob. Any time you feel like helping, jump right in.'

'So I guess this isn't a good time to talk about that kiss?'

'What...?' She held his gaze. He watched the temptation to soften flicker across her eyes, the desire to talk about what was simmering between them, the determination not to. 'No. Never will be.'

She folded her arms over her chest and stared into middle distance as if something really important had snatched her focus. Then she gasped and stalked up to one of the players. 'Joseph. Is that...?' she hissed, obviously trying not to alert the circling media to the crisis. 'A hip flask? Give it to me. No alcohol. You know the rules.'

Okay, backup needed. Knowing how much the success of this trip meant to Dani, and knowing when to call a halt to high jinks, Zac stepped in. He took the silver canister out of the flanker's hand and slipped it into his pocket. His good humour failing fast. 'What the hell are you doing? Where did you get this? You know it's out of bounds.'

Joseph shrugged. But his eyes flitted over to his wife, and back. Before Zac could intervene Dani was at her sister's side. Or rather, in her sister's face. 'You brought this for him? Well, thanks for the support.'

Desere flicked her hand nonchalantly. 'Let loose a little, sis. I was trying to help. He's missing me and needs to chill out. Like you.'

Clearly her sister didn't realise the importance of this for Daniella. 'Desere, alcohol is strictly banned. The others are bound to get jealous if Joseph flouts the rules. That could cause a ruck and bad morale.'

'Yes, Zac. I know. I'm very sorry.' She pouted and for a second Zac really thought she meant it. But the light in her eyes belied her true feelings. Like her father, Desere said the right things but you never quite knew what was going on behind the eyes.

Whereas Daniella was so different; everything she felt or thought was written on her face plain as day. And, weird, he kind of just knew with her. Knew when to get close, knew when to back off. When to kiss her. When to tease. Knew how much she wanted him. How much she pretended not to.

He'd never had that before. Understood someone so completely. It was unnerving and comforting at the same time. And he didn't know what to do with it. Walking away was proving all kinds of difficult.

Desere's pout changed to a smile. 'And sex is banned too, that right, Dani?' Her pupils flared like she was sharing some kind of private joke. She tapped the side of her nose. 'But we both know we can get round it if we want to...'

From where he was standing he could see Dani's hands fisting at her sides. She closed her eyes as red seeped into her cheeks. No—slammed into her cheeks, ears, tip of her nose.

She stepped forward, her shoulders rigid. Her mouth a thin taut line. And he wrestled down the need to speak out for her. The need to help. But what he knew of Dani so far was that she wouldn't thank him for fighting her battles. No matter how painful it was to be on the sideline.

'Just go, Desere, before the press get a hold of this. You're making things ten times worse. And, while you're at it, stop interfering in my life. I don't want to see you until final day. You got it? Go.'

Then she turned and stepped onto the boat without looking back.

He took the place next to her, the seating so tight he had full side-on contact with her body. Felt the simmering anger shake through her, the swell of her breast on every ragged intake of breath. Felt the touch of her knee against his, the pressing of her thigh. Inhaled her sweet smell. Angry, happy, everything he experienced was coloured with her. She even made the regulation navy coverall look sexy. Drove him nuts.

So, okay, maybe he could help her. Keep a satisfactory distance, but help, like a colleague would. Like he should have helped Tom. Yeah, like a friend would. It wouldn't mean anything more, anything deeper. He'd help, then get the hell out.

She barely lifted her eyes to meet his, watched as each of the team scrambled, jumped or dived into the boat. 'Bloody Desere. God only knows who else drank that stuff. Look at Jaxon. Doing stupid things.' She craned her neck and indicated their star player, standing on the deck of the boat. Arms outstretched behind Manu, they were *doing a Titanic*, screaming, 'My heart will go ooooon.'

'So which one's supposed to be Kate Winslet? I don't think Manu's got the ass for it.'

Underneath her frown Zac glimpsed the beginnings of a

smile. The frosting was starting to melt. She nudged him. 'Stop making me laugh. I'm trying to be cross with Desere. Indulge me.'

If only.

He took a chance to squeeze her hand under the folds of the nylon coverall, understanding that regardless of her brave face she must be hurting somewhere. Her sister had directly contravened the very rules Dani was trying to uphold. But she'd slammed her defences up and needed to feel in control. That was the kind of thing he did too. He got that. But understanding it didn't help any. He just wanted to put a smile back on her face. 'I'm sure she didn't mean anything by it. She doesn't know how much this means to you.'

She pulled her hand from his grip. 'Well, she should. Now stop with being nice. I've spent my life fighting Desere. It's just business as usual. Don't you have any siblings you fight with?'

'Yes, a sister, much younger. We might have fought if I'd actually got the chance to spend any time with her. I was shipped off to boarding school when she was still in nappies. School became my family, my home.' Where he'd met the guy he'd considered a brother to him—and then let him down so badly. Guilt sliced through him like a knife. He closed the door on that and focused on Dani. 'Hell, I'm no expert on relationship skills.'

'So we're two of a kind, then, in more ways than one. You enjoyed boarding?'

'Sure. I made a few good mates there.'

'And yet your eyes are saying something else entirely.'

Damn, she was perceptive. He turned away slightly so she couldn't read any more into it. He usually managed to keep a lid on things, and never shared his history past a brief overview. He skirted the subject. 'What was it like at your school?'

'Okay. I get the message. Keep out. I understand if you don't want to go there. My need for privacy is way more than skin-deep too.' She shrugged. 'My school was okay. If it hadn't been for the fact I was a Danatello and following in Desere's footsteps. I had spectacularly glamorous stilet-toes to fill, but I did learn a lot of extracurricular stuff.' She raised her eyebrows.

'Oh? You have skills in other areas?' He leaned closer. 'Show me sometime?'

'Not likely.' Her lips kicked upwards at the corners. 'But you've already seen the photos.'

'Lady Godiva…? You started all that extreme partying at school?'

'Hard not to. A whole lot of rich celeb kids, way too much cash and little regard for authority. But that's all behind me now. I'm a good girl.'

'Sure you are.' The memory of that kiss hovered between them like an invisible thread. Pulling, tightening. She looked up at him through thick black eyelashes and he saw the struggle there. The heat. So now would be a good time to bring the subject up. 'What did Desere mean about the sex ban and *we can get round it*. You told her about the kiss?'

'No.' She glanced around warily, but the boys were dis-tracted by putting on their overalls and finding their seats, and the hum of the engine masked their voices. 'Of course not.'

'The list, then? You've been fishing for suggestions?'

'Get real, Zachary. You're not the subject of my conver-sations.' He guessed the tone was meant to deter him. But it ratcheted his attraction instead.

He grinned. 'You know that whole bossy schoolmistress thing is kind of sexy.'

She put her fingers in her ears. 'Not listening.'

'I have an idea.' Pulling one hand away he leaned into

her ear. Inhaled the sweet smell of her shampoo. 'We could play schools. I could be really naughty and you could give me ten strokes of the cane.'

'Tempting…but not for the reasons you're thinking.'

This was more like it. Sexy Dani. Feisty Dani. He hated that her family had such a subduing effect on her, and that she was still so hell-bent on getting their approval. 'Or we could do hospitals. I could listen to your chest.'

'We're not going to play anything, Zac. Or do anything.' Her voice held a warning, but her eyes…hell, her eyes told him exactly what she wanted—steel determination, warmth. Desire. Definitely to play. Definitely more. Everything.

Shaking her head, her shoulders rigid, she lifted her chin, just enough to show him she had complete control and meant business. 'As gorgeous and irresistible as you may believe yourself to be I'm not in the market for anything. What we did was simply a temporary lapse of judgement.'

'A temporary lapse? Hey, come on, you're not issuing a press statement. How about you use words that actually mean what you're feeling.'

And what was with these intense feelings of his own? Usually the kiss-offs left him with a sense of relief. Not growing frustration. Damn it, he did want to kiss her again. And he certainly didn't want her to be ending it. His male pride was taking a bashing, along with something else—regret, perhaps? Something that made him feel like he'd lost a precious chance. Even though it had to be the best thing for them both. Hell, she'd said exactly what he'd been thinking.

Although his line had been more like *maybe sometime…* not *never again.*

'You're right. I'm sorry. I forgot I was dealing with you. Small words.' She looked into his eyes and gave him a smile suitable for a six-year-old. 'Here's the easy version, Zac. Kissing you was bad.'

'Bad? Bad? I hardly got started.' He sucked in air. 'We could do a replay. See how really bad we could be?'

He watched as her whole body trembled and she bit the corner of her bottom lip. His gaze was drawn to the rich red colour they were today, how they were parted just an inch. Just enough to slip his tongue in. God, he wanted to be so bad with her.

'In your dreams, sunshine.' She rolled her eyes. 'Poor Zachary. Not used to being turned down? Women usually flocking to sleep with you?'

'No…yes.' However he answered he was on a hiding to nothing. 'Let's just say I have a high success rate.'

She laughed. 'I bet you have. But I'm not going to be a notch on any bedpost. So save your energy for the two thousand condoms and your poor unsuspecting next conquest.'

The skipper began his health and safety talk and the boat purred out of the harbour. As they carved through the sparkling Hauraki waters she splashed water over him. At the sharp curve of the three-sixty-degree spin under the stunning iron harbour bridge she leaned forward so he'd get the full force of the spray.

When she tipped her head back and laughed she looked breathtakingly beautiful. If not a little wicked. Where the hell had the meek girl on the red carpet gone? Or the sexy woman in the lift? Dani was all kinds of everything, determined, feisty, vulnerable. And was getting too complicated and hard to resist.

As the boat docked he jumped to the decking and helped with the mooring rope. 'And now you're not even going to let me help you off the boat?'

'I have feet. And a great sense of balance.' She stepped off and ignored his outstretched hand. Two players bounded from behind her jostling and laughing, almost giving her an early ducking in the water. Next the team prop charged past carrying Jaxon on his back. 'Ouch. Watch it!'

Zac grabbed her arm and pulled her into the shadows of a tall boatshed, into safety and out of the glare of the sun— and the waiting media. So close his nose nuzzled in her hair. That damned smell again. Drove him crazy. He kept his hand on her arm, stroked a finger along the bare skin. Felt her shiver in response. 'So much for the balance. You sure you don't want a replay? Later?'

'Zac, d-don't. We need to stop them, they're doing pig-gyback races up the gangplank.'

Okay, so he grinned at the stutter. Nothing like a bit of sex talk to fluster a girl. The more turned on she became, the more the fire raged in his groin. The more he wanted to explore her. He laughed. 'It's fine. Let them unwind a little. Where's your sense of fun?'

'I'm saving it for the day after finals day. When I know I won't be seeing you again. In the meantime we're going to have to think of something to tell those paparazzi over there.' She held out a pretend microphone. 'Dr Price, why are the most highly paid rugby team in New Zealand behav-ing like a bunch of overgrown children on a sugar rush?'

'Good that you asked that, Ms Danatello.' Zac spoke into her fist. 'It's because their minders are contemplating hav-ing sex-free sex in the boatshed.'

'Speak for yourself.'

'In another life, another time, would you?' He leaned in and whispered, 'Because I would. No hesitation.'

She held his gaze. 'I...I don't know.'

But her eyes did the talking. He stood looking at her, mesmerised by the heat in her pupils. He wanted her too much, not just to bed—but more than that. More than he'd wanted any woman for a long time. When had this become so hot he didn't know how to handle it?

Suddenly there was a roar of male voices that had him refocusing. 'Doc. Dani. Can you help?'

His heart regulated as he dropped the play and dashed out to find the prop and Jaxon in a tangled heap on the floor.

CHAPTER SIX

'IF YOU HADN'T been playing the fool we could have saved Jaxon from this. Saved him from himself.' From their quiet corner sofa Dani pointed to the glum-looking lad sitting at the other end of the bar of their Rotorua hotel. His foot, although bandaged and elevated for three days, was still badly swollen. Guilt eked away at her. 'A two-game stand down at least. I only hope it gets better before the semis—if we even get that far without him.'

'And this is my fault how? He's a grown man who makes his own decisions. I didn't drop him on his ankle, then throw my one-hundred-and-twenty-kilogram body on it.' Zac's smile could have charmed the hardest of souls.

But she worked hard at not letting it get to her. 'You should have had more control of them. Their behaviour was unacceptable.'

'And we're here now making sure none of them drink anything stronger than orange juice. Penance doubled. Besides, I was distracted.' His gaze wandered over her mouth, down to her neck, then further to her open-neck blouse. His smile was all sex and promises.

Since the boat ride they'd settled into an unwritten state of eternal flirting. And she was all out of trying to be cross with him, trying to fight off the feelings that he aroused in her. She allowed a smile. It was fun. It was harmless. It never stepped over the line she'd drawn. 'And so now it's my fault?'

'If only you'd stop looking good enough to eat.' He lifted her knuckles to his lips and she stifled a gasp.

'Zac!' About that line she'd drawn… 'Not here.'

'No one's looking, they're playing cards. They can't even see us in this dark corner.' With a wicked grin he opened her palm and brought it to his mouth. Shock waves spiralled through her as he held her gaze. 'Now, how about licking? All over. Starting here. You can tell me where to stop.'

'Stop.'

'Hey, play fair. I've hardly started.'

'First, I'd like to have a conversation that doesn't revolve around sex.'

'Why?'

'I don't usually lick people I don't know very well.'

'You know me. Zac. Doctor. Demon kisser.'

She frowned. 'And yet when I ask about anything that's deeper than a paper cut you change the subject.'

'I do not.' Now his tongue ran tiny circles over the tender skin on her palm. Heat coiled in the pit of her stomach, spreading down through her abdomen. The intent in his eyes was dangerous.

'Stop the licking already.'

'Okay.' He wrapped her hand in both of his, took a steadying breath. For once he was serious. 'What do you want to know?'

'School. What's the score? What happened?'

He visibly paled. A mix of emotions flitted across his face—the most real she'd seen him—no mask of sexuality or professionalism to hide behind. He looked raw and that socked her in the chest. 'Nothing. It was a long time ago. I don't talk about it.'

'And now you do. See. Easy.' At the blank look on his

face she relented. Surprising that someone as bright and breezy as Zac had dark corners he didn't want exploring. 'Okay. Don't worry, I get it. I don't want the whole story— not if you don't feel able to tell me. But let me in a little. Life's not all about sex and lists….'

'Aha.' He looked relieved at the mention of the damned list. 'But the list is now. We have now and we have tomorrow. After that…then the chaos begins.'

'Jeez, Zac, do I have to spell it out? No talking, no list.'

'You Danatellos drive such a hard bargain.' He thought for a while—trying to gauge how much to tell her, she imagined. Shadows blew in behind his eyes. He looked lost. Not the gregarious funny guy she'd grown to care for. Confident Zac was struggling and she desperately wanted to help. Knew well enough that he wouldn't accept anything from her. But there it was. She'd grown to care for him. Whatever that meant. 'Try me.'

Zac's eyebrows raised. 'Okay. Short version. I had a good friend and I let him down. I should have been there for him and I wasn't. It's the only thing I've ever regretted.'

'I know a lot about regret.'

'And about living again.' He brushed his hands down his jeans and stood, looked around the now empty bar. 'Okay, that's enough. This lot have cleared off. I think it's time to get going.'

'But…'

'I said, enough.' The shutters were back behind his eyes.

She'd pushed too far. Pried in places she wasn't welcome. He needed space. 'Sure. I'll just see if there are any messages at reception before I turn in. See you in the morning.'

'Sleep well, princess.' He looked at her apologetically, then dipped his head towards her and placed a kiss on her cheek. It was such a sweet gesture—uncalculated and laden with a sadness that she'd unwittingly evoked in him—it

tugged at her heart. So unexpected to see him like that—
a glimpse into what made him so whole. If only she could
stop him becoming so much more than a colleague. If only
she could stop thinking about that damned list.

A loud buzzing jolted Zac out of a dream he didn't want to
wake up from. Involving him and Dani and lots of...oh, yes,
lots of... He glanced at the LED clock display. One-thirty.
    There it was again. Buzzing. His phone on vibrate? He
grabbed it from the nightstand and squinted at the message.

Zac? Is Matt awake? D.

    What the...? A text from Dani. At way too late...or early.
The middle of the night.
    He didn't need to glance over to the huddle in the next
bed. The loud stuffed-pig snoring told him that, after com-
plaining too loudly and too long about his indigestion, Matt
was away with the sleep fairies. Zac read the text again to
decipher its meaning. Why did she want to know if Matt
was awake? He tried to join the dots but the blood hadn't
made its journey back up to his brain.
    Fact: she'd texted him. At bedtime.

No. He's sleeping like a babe, why?

    Why, indeed?
    Hey, hey. A sudden rush of heat rebounded back to his
groin. Surely there could only be one reason she'd text him
at this time of night?

Good. I need you. Now. D.

    Needed as in to kill a creepy-crawly? Needed as in she
had an itch she wanted him to scratch? Holy moly. She

wanted to play? Musical beds. What other reason would a woman want him for at this time of night? His imagination took over from where his dream had left off. Her blonde curls pooled over the pillow, long suntanned legs wrapped around his. Her shimmer-covered eyes closed, head thrown back, in a bed very similar to the one he was in. Less than ten feet away.

You sure, Dani?

Absolutely. Can you come now?

Whoa. He could. But for the small matter of the sex ban. If Davide or Matt found out he'd be crucified. His hand hovered over the phone keypad. Was this some kind of test? Her father trying to freak him out? Dani taking things up a notch?

Despite the playing, the flirting and the kiss, they'd both agreed on not taking this any further. Spending the night was way further and then some. Then she'd started asking questions he didn't want to answer, probing deeper than he was prepared to go. Crazy thing was, he'd been tempted to tell her. But that would have been a step closer, allowing her in. He couldn't risk his future on falling for someone like her. Someone who'd depend on him, who'd need him to be there. Someone who he'd inevitably let down.

But heck, the woman needed him right now. Who was he to turn down a cry for help?

Zac? PLEASE COME NOW.

Down, Tonto. He felt the hot sting of arousal intensify. Okay, plan A—he'd make sure she was safe, then he'd come back to bed.

Plan B—he'd make sure she was safe, talk to her about

boundaries, make his stance clear. No ties. No commitment. Maybe fool around a bit, then come back to bed.

Anything to help out a damsel in distress.

He slipped out of bed, careful not to wake Sleeping Beauty. No sex didn't mean no fun. They could have fun coming up with new things to add to the list. And Matt need never know. He could be out and back in a few…hours.

He carefully pulled open the drawer full of condoms. Safety first. Ribbed? Flavoured? Extra sensitive? Sure, he was a sensitive kind of guy. He grabbed a fistful of brightly coloured foil.

On my way, princess. Brace yourself. ;-)

Shucking on jeans and a hoodie he tiptoed to the door and creaked it open. The corridor was deserted. One glance towards her room had his heart pounding and mouth watering. The door behind him clicked closed. The noise echoed off the pale tea-coloured walls.

Shoot. He checked his hoodie pockets. Essentials: Phone. Check. Condoms. Check. Key? Damn. And now he was locked out.

His phone vibrated again.

Thank you, Zac. I'm in the bar. Come quickly. I can't do this on my own.

What? His stomach tightened into a knot. Not bed? The bar?

Cursing, he stalked to the lift. Why was she still in the bar at this time in the morning? None of it made sense.

He punched the lift button to Ground. *I can't do this on my own.* What did it mean? She was in trouble? And out of all the people on the team she'd contacted him. Either she trusted him, or she didn't trust anyone else.

She was sitting at the bar wearing the same tracksuit as earlier, twiddling a beermat. Either she hadn't bothered to leave the place or she'd come back for some reason. A bartender stood at the end of the bar, dishcloth in hand, wiping at a glass. Cheesy elevator music played in the background. It was like a scene from a seedy movie.

'Dani, what's going on?'

She pointed to the foils he'd stupidly kept in his fist. 'Really? A woman asks you for help in the dead of night and you automatically assume she wants sex?'

He stuffed the condoms into his pocket. 'She usually does.'

'Sorry to disappoint you, Mr Hefner, but this is a boutique hotel in Rotorua, not Playboy Mansion....'

'What are you doing here at this time of night?'

'I was going to the gym for a work-out.' She frowned. 'Couldn't sleep. Saw the light, heard the noise, a familiar voice.'

She swivelled on the stool and pointed to the unlit corner they'd been sitting in a few hours before. Through the dark Zac made out a shape. A large first-five shape. 'And discovered we have a problem.'

'Jaxon?'

'Jaxon. We thought he'd gone up to bed with the rest of the team.' She slipped off the stool and went to crouch at the player's slumped side, took his pulse and counted his resps. 'C.J., the barman, tells me he careered back in here a few hours ago cursing and shouting at first, disappointed with his two-game stand down. Seems he finished off the contents of his minibar and then came down here to continue his little binge. The booze has now started to work its magic. He's been asleep for a while. Lucky for him I found him and not anyone else.'

A loud snore emanated from the player's nose.

Zac bit back another curse. 'Your father's going to kill him.'

'No, he isn't.' At his raised eyebrows she shrugged. 'We're not going to tell him.'

'Like hell we're not. The place is probably crawling with CCTV cameras. And see him, there? C.J.? One word from him and it'll be all over the papers. We need transparency and honesty. And a good PR firm.'

She shook her head. 'No. We'll have to take a risk on the cameras. C.J.'s agreed to keep quiet. For a small sum.' She'd got it all worked out. Bribery, lies and manipulation. Another normal day in the Danatello household.

'So we pretend this never happened? Keep it from Mr I-don't-like-secrets? Great. Fabulous. I'd prefer a *walk away and pretend I'd never been here* kind of plan.'

She lifted her head and threw him the kind of look his mother used to give him when he'd disappointed her. Again. 'Oh, of course. Forget poor Jaxon. You need to keep your job. Right?'

'Why do you say it like it's some kind of dirty sin? I've lived and breathed hard work to get to this. With a lot of consequences.' And he didn't feel much like explaining any more.

He blew out a breath. Things had been going so well. The future had finally looked bright. A great job. If the team won, the bonus he'd receive would be awesome, enough to make things stable for another few years. Enough to make him believe that some good had come out of what had happened.

Dani wound her hair round her finger. Something he hadn't seen her do for a while. When he put his hand on hers she gave him a small smile of thanks. Wrapped her fingers into his. 'Please think about this, Zac. You can't let one small slip-up affect Jaxon's career. The problem is, he's too rich, has far too much pressure on those young shoulders and now has too much time on his hands to brood. He needs help, not the sack. Come on, you're a doctor, you can see what he needs.'

'Below the belt, Dani, appealing to my professional nature.'

She blinked. 'It's true though. Medicine's about so much more than physical healing.'

'Yeah and we can get him some good help. Above board. But management need to know about this.'

She shook her head. 'Do they? It's one minor transgression that no one need know about. Didn't you ever do something you regretted?'

Hell, yes. Did she have to needle him right where it hurt? 'This isn't about me.'

'You know what will happen if Daddy finds out. Don't ruin the rest of his life.'

'And this is more about you than about him.' About her experiences, which she shouldn't be bringing into a clinical picture.

'I'm trying to protect him from the kind of thing that happened to me. It's not nice. You should try it sometime.' Her shoulders lifted and she ripped the beermat up and threw the pieces over the stained table. 'You want to know what it's like to be scrutinised and found wanting? For your life to be in bits? For everyone to see you naked on the front page?'

The tone in her voice changed; anger softened with pain pierced his heart. She'd been through hell. Plain and simple. When the world had laughed at her, no one had given a thought to how much it hurt.

'If we cover this up and Davide finds out, he'll sack the

lot of us. We're walking a tight line here.' Even hearing his words made him cringe. And hell, when it came down to it he'd been in a similar situation before. When doing the right thing for one person meant the abjectly wrong thing for someone else.

'But you're not saying no, right?'

When he didn't answer she sucked in a breath, exhaled slowly. She stood and paced back and forth. 'Okay. What about patient confidentiality? You made an oath. You're not *allowed* to tell anyone about this. Even if the management, the press and the nation all believe they own a piece of him, they don't. He has as much right to privacy as anyone else.'

'And if your father does get wind of this? What happens then for you?'

That seemed to sway her a little. He knew just how much getting her father's affection meant to her. And she'd be taking a huge risk; he didn't want her to fail on such a scale.

But she shook her head. 'I know what risk I'm running here. I've endured worse. It's okay, I'll take the rap for it.'

The look she gave him now was devoid of emotion—as if she expected him to let her down like everyone else in her life. And he knew at that moment he'd do anything to wipe that look from her eyes.

It still didn't feel right, but what choice did he have? 'Okay. Then we need to get him out of this public area for a start. Who is he sharing with?'

'Manu. But we can't take him back there. The fewer people who know, the better. And anyway, he's going to need babysitting for the next few hours.' Now she was the most serious he'd ever seen her. 'Alcohol poisoning is horrible. But getting through it on your own is even worse.'

He shoved his shoulder into Jaxon's armpit and levered him upright. 'Mine, then? No, Matt's there. Yours?'

'Yes, it'll have to be.' She took Jaxon's other arm. 'We can watch him in shifts. Okay?'

Despite every part of him telling him this was crazy, he edged their patient to the lift and then shuffled him towards Dani's room. Once they'd put him into the recovery position and secured bowl, bucket and towels Zac looked round for Dani. She was reaching into the wardrobe for spare duvets so they could be comfortable as they took it in turns to watch their patient.

This was so not what he'd had in mind when he'd dreamt about spending the night with her.

'Thank you. I mean it.' Dani handed the duvet down to Zac. She'd watched him struggle with his decision to help her, and seen how much it had cost him. And she couldn't shake the thought he'd done it for her. Not for Jaxon. This was new ground—someone who put themselves on the line to help her. New and shaky, and she didn't know how to process the warmth it gave her. Sure, he was funny, smart and now…loyal. She had to keep reminding herself he was also holding things back and very, very temporary in her life. So distance was called for. 'Why don't you get some rest. I'll take first watch until four-thirty, you can do until seven.'

'And where do you propose we rest with our guest taking up the king-size?' He smiled. 'At least my room is a twin.'

'And occupied. Talking of which, what are you going to tell Matt about where you spent the night? He could get the completely wrong idea.'

The smile wavered. 'I don't know. And I locked myself out too.'

'Typical.' She laughed. 'I don't know who's worse. You or our friend here. Your brain is hot-wired for sex, not sense.'

'Hey…I didn't know I was going to end up here like this. I came to help…'

'You came for sex.'

'Okay…' he conceded. 'Might have been on the agenda. You seriously need to make yourself clearer in your texts. I'll make something up…say I went for a swim. Or a walk.'

'With a lifetime supply of condoms?'

He frowned. 'There's ten. Not much of a life.'

'I was thinking it was more than enough. For you.'

'I get my fair share. Don't you worry.' He inhaled sharply. 'With a bit of luck Matt will still be asleep and won't even know I've been missing. I can get a new swipe card from reception. Surely?'

Why did it feel like they were breaking every rule in the book? And why was it so exciting? Her heart danced a little jig and every part of her felt alive. Their jobs were on the line; and right now her body didn't seem to give a damn about that.

'Okay, you can deal with that early tomorrow, after sleep has doused your sex drive and you have a working brain cell or two.' She glanced around the room. Nice decor, shame about the lack of anything for two people to sleep on. 'How about the chaise longue? We can top and tail. Unless you want the bath.' *Please take the bath.* Up close and personal without meaningful contact was not on her bucket list. But then neither was imagining him using those condoms with someone other than her.

She shuddered. Spending time with Zac was like a lesson in emotional states. She'd gone from wired to regretful, irritated and now jealous. Of someone who existed purely in her imagination.

Don't even mention aroused. Aroused could not be on the menu. Although it was there. More there than anything else. Jeez, she was too confused by her over-enthusiastic hormones and the craziness of having not one but two men for an unscheduled sleepover to think straight.

He took the duvet from her and threw it over the chaise. 'We'll take that, at least it has padding.' Then he shoved the piece of ornate furniture against the wall. 'You take the end with the backrest. I'll prop myself up against the wall.'

'Thanks. See, you can be nice when you try.' She plumped up two large white pillows and threw him one. Aiming at his head, but he caught it swiftly, winked and popped it on his side of the chaise. *His side.*

'I aim to please.'

'Well, you do. I suppose. Sometimes.'

'Wow, Dani. Don't get carried away with the praise.'

'Trust me, I won't.' Grabbing her nightgown she ducked into the bathroom and got ready for bed. All the time hyper-aware that spending the night with Zac, even under strange circumstances, was a bad idea. A good bad idea. A delicious bad idea. And dumb in the extreme. But what choice did she have?

She opened the door a crack. 'I'm coming out now, close your eyes.'

'When?' He smiled as she stepped into the room pulling her nightgown down to cover her knees. Why hadn't she brought sensible flannelette PJs instead of this red satin number?

'Now!'

'Oops. Too late. I forgot.' He spluttered. 'Whoa! What are you wearing?'

His eyes grew wide as his gaze travelled from her neck to her cleavage, down her body—slowly…excruciatingly slowly, past her hips to her knees. His smile grew warm, hot. Very hot.

She clutched her wash-bag to her chest—as if that would hide either her embarrassment or the flare in her eyes that she knew was there. Fire shot to her belly.

'You're supposed to have your eyes closed.'

'And miss this? No way.' He shucked off his hoodie and wrapped it over her shoulders. 'But put this on. If Jaxon wakes up and sees you in that flimsy thing you'll give him a heart attack on top of his hangover.'

Ignoring the heat and his smell enveloping her she shrugged the hoodie off and glared at him. 'I'm going to be under a duvet. What's he going to see? Besides, not everyone has the same one-track mind as you.'

'Darling, believe me, everyone would be on this track if they saw you in that. That's some serious lingerie.'

'It's one of my vices. A hangover from school.' She climbed under the duvet, her cheeks burning and heart ramping up to overdrive. She had to spend the night with him and somehow survive, so her raging heart could damn well stop raging and go back to slow and steady. Thank you.

He looked at the deep V of lace-trimmed silk covering her cleavage. 'No one ever wore anything like that at my boarding school.'

'Clearly you didn't have unwritten bitch contests to see who had the most money, the most famous parents or on-trend clothes, like at mine.' She shuddered as she remembered those hideous days, the catfights and false friendships. 'Petty rivalry even went as far as bed wear.'

'No, no bitch contests and definitely no sexy lingerie at mine.' She searched his face for the shadows, but clearly he was remembering better school times. His eyes glittered as he laughed. 'It was all boys for a start.'

'You are such a jerk, Zachary.' So the man had a zillion different sides and she liked them all. The one that agreed to put his own job on the line to help her, the one who wanted to protect her no matter how much she didn't need him to. The one who made her laugh. The one who was easy to talk to.

He was becoming more and more of a problem. His smell,

the memory of his taste, his smile, those broad shoulders. That wicked twinkle in his eyes. Not to mention the darned dimple. All taunted her like off-limits treats.

It was too hard to imagine what life was going to be like beyond the tournament. Beyond this. Could men and women be friends? Just friends? Or did the sex thing always get in the way?

Right now, as he sidled in opposite her wearing nothing but a pair of black boxers and a killer smile, the sex thing was raising its hand screaming, *Pick me*.

She drew her eyes away from his hard wall of chest, the defined pecs and smattering of jet-black hair that made him even more man, and found her voice.

'I'll keep this side light on if you don't mind. It'll make it easier to keep an eye on our pal over there. I think I'll read to keep myself awake.' She waved her physiotherapy text book at him and opened the chapter on iliotibial band injury management.

They both jumped as Jaxon snorted, sniffled and groaned. Then settled back to sleep.

'Go for your life. And I hope you don't make as much noise as him when you're asleep.' Zac wriggled under the duvet, his toes reaching up to her thigh. She edged away from him as he folded the pillow under his head and closed his eyes. From this angle she watched the slow rise and fall of his chest, the flutter of his dark long eyelashes against his cheek. And felt her blood pound round her body with such force it made her feel dizzy. Just friends? Who was she trying to kid? Just friends was impossible, but more than friends was impossible too.

Silence stretched across the night. His breathing became rhythmical, doing the off beat to Jaxon's four-four-time snuffling. She sighed and started to relax.

'Iliotibial band syndrome...' was not holding her attention.

Suddenly his foot tapped gently against her leg. 'Talk to me.'

'Shouldn't you be sleeping now?' She tried to squeeze away from him but there was nowhere to go.

'Oh, yes. Forgot. Right.' He closed his eyes again and grinned. 'But I'll go to sleep way quicker if you talk to me. A bedtime story?'

'How old are you?'

His grin broadened. 'It could include potential list items...I hear erotica is all the rage. I'll leave it open.'

'No lists. No funny stuff. We are not alone, remember?'

'With that noise I'm not likely to forget.' His toes wriggled against her thigh. 'Spoilsport.'

'One more time and you'll be in the bath.' She huffed out a breath. Loudly. Just so he'd hear the frustration. 'Okay. Once upon a time there was a very irritating man who refused to go to sleep, so his...friend did away with him in a very nasty grisly way. With lots of blood and pain.' She tweaked his toe. Hard. 'The end.'

'Don't ever take up writing for your next career. You really suck.'

'No fear, I'll stick to twisting limbs. Much more fun.'

'So you have an evil side too. Very interesting...you are very interesting, Daniella.' He laughed and opened his eyes. Heat from his body curled around hers. His smile kicked up one corner of his mouth, making his dimple twinkle. He looked for a second like a mischievous child.

He watched her for a while, but slowly his expression changed to thoughtful. He pushed back against the wall and sat up. 'Hey, princess. Tell me about that photograph. What was going on back then?'

'Why are you asking?' She drew her legs up in an effort to wriggle away from him, wrapped her arms around her knees. She was so not ready for this.

'You were so angry down there tonight, thought it might help if you talked a bit.' He leaned forward.

'Oh, yeah. The big guy who won't talk wants me to talk. Right.'

He took her hand. 'I'm trying to help. Maybe build a bit of trust here. Reckon we could both use it.'

'No.' Her reaction was automatic. She couldn't hold in the tight bitter laugh as she snatched her hand away. 'I don't trust any man, not least one who's employed by my father.'

'I'm a man. And I'm employed by your father. Can you separate the two?' He held his palms out to her. 'You keep harping on about talking. Go on, try me.'

She sat there watching his face in the half-light, remembering the thunderous look when he'd arrived in the bar all breathless and confused. All she'd been able to think about was how the heck to save Jaxon, but all Zac had been concerned about was saving her.

Well, actually, it had been about sex. But he'd stayed and helped. To save her—the younger her. To prove someone cared.

That he would do that for her—

Something shifted inside her, swelled and filled a hole she hadn't realised had been there. For so long she'd kept her own counsel, hadn't let anyone in, but maybe it would feel good to let that go just for a few minutes. Trouble was she didn't know if she could, and now was not a good time to learn to trust a man. Right when he was going to walk out of her life in a matter of weeks.

But hell, if she wanted him to open up to her, she had to lead the way. Just a bit—after all, touching on details wasn't baring her soul, right?

'They were wild, crazy days. We had too much time on our hands and too much money to blow on booze and dope.'

She nodded towards Jaxon. 'Like Numpty here. Getting wasted was our number-one priority.'

'Our? We?'

'My friends.' As she said it she rolled her eyes and made speech mark shapes with her fingers. Zac got the impression that people like the Danatellos didn't have friends. They had hangers-on, wannabes. 'People who I trusted and who let me down. People who sold me out when I was in rehab. Paul.'

'Paul?'

'My ex-fiancé, who only wanted to marry me to get to Davide. Oh, not just him. Others. People on Daddy's payroll…'

Like him. Things cleared a little in Zac's muddled brain. No wonder she'd put up barriers. Everyone she'd trusted had let her down. Still let her down if he counted Desere. And yeah, he was counting.

His hands twisted in the duvet. He hated that she'd been used like that. That people had stepped over her, that he hadn't been there to help. He wanted to show her that not everyone was like them. That he…that he what? That he could offer her something else? Something more?

He swallowed deeply. What could he offer her?

She paused and seemed to close down a little even now when they were in bed together. She started to wrap her hair round her finger.

He reached out and unwound the curl, held her fingers in his. Took the chance to look deep into her eyes and found some small element of trust there, despite what she said. But heck, she was fighting it. 'Stop chewing your hair, Daniella.'

'I'll do what I damn well like,' she fired at him, but let her fingers drop. 'I was pretty pathetic back then. The kind of person I have little time for now. I had no ambition, no skills except in how to party hard, and how to fall even harder. And boy, did I fall.'

'The photo.' He thought about his life and how ordered he'd made it. He'd had a plan from an early age of escaping the disapproval of his parents, of being single-minded and determined. The only thing he'd ever wanted was to be a doctor and he'd made that happen—albeit at a heavy cost. But Dani had done the opposite to him; there'd been no plan at all. Just chaos.

She nodded. 'That stupid Lady Godiva moment was the best wake-up call I ever had. Although I didn't think so at the time. I was crushed. Mortified. My father threw money at *the problem* to make it go away. I promised him a month at the Inner Sanctum in return for bail. Funny thing was, I really was exhausted—I was tired of living like that. Tired of everything.'

Zac nodded. He'd seen the photo—and despite the naked image of her beautiful body, he'd recognised the vacant expression, the blank eyes, the total lack of emotion.

And yet, she'd dragged herself into a profession, learnt useful skills and faced the world again. Stepping onto that red carpet in front of those cameras had taken far more courage than he would ever have.

Sitting here swamped by the king-size duvet she looked so small, but inside her there was a nugget of strength so pure and proud it shone.

Her eyes widened as she fixed a smile. 'And that's where the story ends for tonight. They all lived happily ever after. Time for sleep.'

'Like I'll manage to get any with you here.'

'Don't, Zac. Please.'

The warning was valid. Each conversation was a step closer to intimacy that neither of them could risk.

He tried hard to banish the raging erotic thoughts zooming round his brain. It would be so easy to kiss her, too easy. Her mouth was just inches away, those soft supple lips within reach. But that would lead to other things—perhaps—would certainly lead to her edging closer into his heart. And he couldn't take that, couldn't get ensnared in a web of promises he couldn't keep. Dani deserved better; she deserved someone who would be there for her, to cherish her. He couldn't start something that could only end in disaster.

Which, considering he was under a duvet with her, half naked, was a joke.

He was already in way too deep.

CHAPTER SEVEN

DAYLIGHT FILTERED THROUGH a chink in the thick fern-green curtains, Dani squinted and shifted. Her left leg had gone numb, her neck felt acutely displaced and something heavy lay across her chest. She sniffed and got the divine scent of Zac. Heat prickled through her. No. So inappropriate. But lovely.

Reason began to seep into her groggy brain. Her leg had no feeling because his leg was squashing it. Her nose was filled with his smell because her nostril was flat up against the dip in his neck. Somehow she'd fallen asleep at one end of the chaise, but woken at the other. Entwined, not just in his arms, but his legs too. She glanced over to the bed. How much had Jaxon seen, or read into this? For that matter, how much had Zac read into this?

Opening up to him had been purging and a relief—but, in the cold light of day, had she told him too much? She'd never poured her heart out to anyone on that level before. So that made her a trusting fool or just plain desperate. Either way she wouldn't be doing it again. She didn't want anyone knowing enough to go to the papers. Experience told her he'd get a pretty penny for dishing the dirt on her. Experience also told her no matter how much a man got her to trust him, he always broke it in the end.

No sign of Jaxon, but the sound of rushing water meant he must be taking a shower. Great, no lasting damage from his ill-judged pity party. But boy, she had a lot to say to him this morning.

Starting with a hefty dose of tough love.

Levering Zac's arm from her chest she wriggled sideways to the edge of the bed. Leaving him was hard, but staying would be so much harder in the end.

'Bye,' she whispered into the duvet.

'Hey, come back.' He grunted, pulled her closer, then continued to snore gently. What was it with these men and snoring? She waited a few seconds until he'd drifted back off, then wriggled again.

He wriggled back in rhythm. Something hard and hot jabbed into her thigh.

No.

God. No. Please. Not here. Not him. Not this.

She swallowed deeply, refusing to acknowledge the tingles of electricity firing through her body, the shot of awareness in her abdomen. The temptation to run her fingers over his lips, to hold him, taste him again, almost overwhelmed her.

This could not be happening. She could not want to touch Zac, to lie here in his arms and imagine what he'd feel like inside her.

She couldn't want to kiss him again, so much that she had a physical ache. Or to enjoy the slice of joy in her heart at waking up next to him.

You are a physio for the Auckland Jets. He is the doctor. You have been caring for a client together. No more.

Her body shook with the desire racing along her veins. How easy it would be to take him in her hands and pull him into her. Would that be all kinds of wrong?

Of course it would.

Trying to control her breathing she turned carefully to face him, all the better to edge her bottom out of the covers, away from his…away from him. She stole a quick look at his face. Her heart swelled at the sight of him. His mouth curved in a tiny smile, thick eyelashes brushing his cheeks. Beautiful. Annoying in so many ways, but beautiful too.

She needed perspective and space. A long walk, a jog, a damned marathon. Whatever it took to shake off this feeling. But she was stuck here. She couldn't go anywhere until Jaxon vacated the bathroom. Above everything else she needed to check on her patient.

'Good morning, princess.' Zac's eyes fluttered open and a long slow grin spread across his face. He waggled his hips and erection towards her. Which was both horrifying and delicious at the same time. 'Sometimes you just don't need words.' He didn't even have the decency to look embarrassed.

'And sometimes you just need a cold shower.' Wriggling was over; now she jumped out from under the covers. 'It's high time we got dressed.'

'Well, that's a shame.' He lazily rolled over onto his back. His hair was dishevelled and he had the tiniest of crinkles round his eyes. Why did he seem to get more gorgeous the more she looked at him? 'We could have had some early-morning exercise.'

'How about a long walk, off a short pier?' She threw her pillow at his head. This time she hit the target with a thwump. 'Do you always wake up so irritatingly fresh?'

'Absolutely. Perky and ready to go.'

'Well, next time don't.'

His grin widened. 'Next time? You mean we get to do this all over again?'

'What? You had fun? Getting very little sleep on a tiny backless couch, clearing up the bodily fluids of a sozzled rugby player and listening to the dulcet strains of the phil-harmonic snoring orchestra?'

'Well, you had most of the duvet, and you spent the night with me... Some women would pay a lot of money for that.'

'Then they have more money than sense.'

'You didn't think that in the lift.'

'You are so delusional.' Gibing, laughing and the promise of sex. Was this how it would be if she woke up with him every morning?

Like that could happen. Guys like Zac didn't do the whole relationship thing. He was a player. Like Paul. Like her father. She doubted he knew what the word *commitment* meant. And most certainly didn't want to lose her heart to that kind of man again.

He sat up and folded his arms across his chest. 'So how is our wonderful patient?'

'Taking too long in the shower.' She shrugged on Zac's hoodie, pulled his condoms from the pocket, tutted loudly at him and threw them in the bin.

'Hey! I might need them.'

'I heard you had plenty more. Bet you didn't have this kind of *sleeping with Dani* on your mind?' Served him right for assuming something so far off kilter.

And yet...she'd opened her heart to him and he'd seemed genuine and caring. She hadn't pegged him as the sensitive type. But he hadn't made a real pass at her, even though they'd been in a prime position to do so. God, the man made her all kinds of confused. Which made her all kinds of angry.

She hammered on the bathroom door. 'Hey, Jaxon, there's a worldwide water shortage. Four-minute showers, please.' She turned and tried not to look at Zac's suntanned chest as she spoke to him. 'How was he on your shift?'

'I nearly contacted noise control to measure his decibels.

There's got to be a health and safety risk there—I should have been issued with earplugs.' He shrugged, twisted round to stand.

'No. Stay there.' There had to be a law against having a body that good. If she had to look at it for any length of time she couldn't trust her actions. 'Duvet up. Thanks.'

Snuggling back under the covers, with a confused look in his eyes, Zac continued, 'He was sick once, then slept the sleep of the dead. Lucky for him we have the morning off. I think he's past the worst, but he'll have a headache from hell this morning. And probably won't feel much like eating for a while.'

'Good.' She crossed the room and picked up the phone receiver. 'Room service? Three full English breakfasts please. Heavy on the grease.'

Zac's eyebrow raised. 'But, Dani...*everyone makes mistakes.*' His mimick of her voice was remarkably good; she almost laughed.

'Yes, well, he's going to pay for his. This is the best way I can think of. Then you, me and him are going to sit down and have a long frank chat about the dangers of alcohol, being a supportive team player and how he put all of our jobs on the line. He needs to pay back.'

'Or pay it forward.' Zac scratched a hand over his morning stubble. He looked pensive for a moment. The soft change in his voice a surprise. 'Do you have plans for this morning? I know we're busy with training, hot pools and that dinner tonight, but we have a few hours.'

In reality she'd planned to run an extra injury clinic, catch up on her notes and have a long hot bubble bath. Some well-earned Zac-free me-time. But suddenly all that faded into... 'Nothing particular. What do you have in mind?'

He frowned, seemed to be battling something in his head. He was formulating a plan. Whatever it was, it involved her.

Her heart rate notched up a gear. He nodded. 'Since these players are supposed to be doing their very best to be good role models to Kiwi kids, and not getting blotto in the bar, you and I are going to take Jaxon on a little trip.'

'Treetops?' Beside Zac, in the passenger seat, Dani pointed to the roadside sign. 'What is this place?'

'It's a respite home for physically challenged kids.' Zac turned the hire car into the long tree-flanked driveway, his grip on the steering wheel tightening along with his chest. A huge brick settled in his throat and threatened his ability to speak. What the hell was he doing?

As if waking up with her in that slinky red satin thing that barely covered her curves, and his very *friendly* full salute, hadn't been foolish enough, coming out to Treetops was probably one of the most stupid things he'd blundered into without thinking.

Bringing an audience to one of his most private places? So private he'd never found the courage to come here himself. And hell, he didn't share this kind of stuff. Didn't want more questions, to relive the dark times.

But after seeing Dani open up a bit he determined to do the same. Give a little. And teach Jaxon a salient life lesson too.

Only, this wasn't opening up, this was laying his soul bare. Something he'd never been able to do before.

Question was, was he ready to give this part of himself?

He dug deep to find his usual jokey repartee but it had done a bunk, so he sucked in a breath and pointed to a cluster of buildings. Even though he'd never visited he knew the layout with his eyes closed. Not one detail had been spared in the planning and he'd overseen it all. From a distance. 'That's the adapted gym and climbing wall. There's also a small cinema chill-out area, a swimming and kayaking pool and, of course, the stables.'

'Stables? Excellent.' Dani's voice was laced with admiration as she looked across the courtyard and beyond to the rolling volcanic hills and Rotorua town in the distance.

From here they could see steam curling into the sky from the thermal pools straight ahead, and to the right, the famous gondola and luge track. Thick lush forest bordered the turquoise lake. Rotorua was a playground for outdoor sports. He wondered whether he should have gone bungee-jumping with the other guys instead. Plunging headfirst hundreds of feet into a dingy chasm seemed much more appealing right now.

But Dani's eyes shone and she looked in awe of the place. Good call. 'When I was training I volunteered at a local stables and helped run the riding-for-disabled programme. I loved it—almost as much as the kids.'

And he loved the way her cheeks had pinked up, her eyes darting around taking it all in. It gave him the power punch he needed.

'Let's get out and I'll show you the rest.' He walked Dani and a trailing Jaxon along the ramps connecting the buildings to a horseshoe courtyard filled with play equipment. 'We had fun choosing these. This modular playzone looks like any regular play park, but it has extrawide seats, a drag ramp and rubberised deck, so any child of any ability can use it. The go-karts are customised—although we still have problems with dangerous drivers.'

Dani nodded, clearly looking over the place with her professional eye. 'Very inclusive—there's something for everyone, regardless of ability.'

'That's the idea.' His attention turned to the large colonial villa, brightly painted in bold primary colours. 'It's meant to be a home from home, just for a few days, or weeks, to give families some fun times. By all accounts the kids love it.'

'By all accounts?'

'We've kept all the thank-you letters on file. I don't get the chance to visit.' Hadn't made the chance to visit. 'Seeing as we're only an hour's drive away I thought we should pop over. I'm sure the children would be thrilled to have Jaxon throw a ball around. What do you say, Jaxon?'

'Sure.' The young lad shrugged and emanated his trademark one-syllable responses. His colour had picked up and, since Dani's inspired breakfast, he'd managed to utter the word *sorry*. But that was all they'd got out of him. He stuck his hands deep in his pockets and looked like he thought heaving into a hotel toilet might be more preferable to being here.

'Zac? Hi. You found us okay?' A familiar deep male voice had him swivelling round. Tom. His heart lifted a little. If he was shocked, angry or surprised to see him here after all this time Tom didn't show it. But then emotion was something he rarely saw on Tom's face—Zac didn't hang around to socialise after the trust board meetings in Auckland.

Zac found a smile, stretched out his hand, unsure as to whether Tom would even take it. 'Good to see you.'

'About time you actually set foot in the place.' Tom lifted his arm from his wheelchair rims and shook. Zac's continued absence from Treetops had been an embarrassment that had turned into an in joke. It was about as close to a laugh together as they got these days. Always, the spectre of that tragic day hung between them. 'Dani, Jaxon, this is Tom, founder and medical resident of Treetops. Tom, these are the special visitors I told you about on the phone.'

Tom nodded and smiled at the pair. His gaze landed on Dani and his eyebrows knotted.

Sure, go ahead and ask. Zac smiled back. *I don't know what the hell we're doing here either.*

Tom seemed to think better than to ask awkward questions; he pushed open the main house door. 'The kids are just finishing off their archery session, then we'll have morning tea and maybe some murderball? What do you say, Jaxon? You up for it?' He looked at Jaxon expectantly. But the young player kept quiet, looking more terrified than taking a match-winning penalty in front of a crowd of sixty thousand.

'It's wheelchair rugby,' Zac explained. 'Maybe you can teach them some ball-handling skills? How to pass off both hands? That'd be a good start.' Zac tried to give Jaxon an encouraging smile. He knew—hoped—that once the whistle blew Jaxon would find some enthusiasm. 'That's before they trounce you in a game.'

Now the talk had turned to something the kid could engage in he did seem to relax a little. Or maybe it was the thought of losing that had blood rushing into his cheeks. 'Okay. I s'pose.'

A riot of noise met them as they wandered through the house towards the dining area and back garden; wide decks opened to boardwalk tracks zigzagging across acres of grassland. Over the hill came eight wheelchairs at full pelt.

'Steady on now! Slow down. We have guests. Don't want to scare them off.' Tom called them all to order and explained over muffins and hot chocolate that Jaxon was here to teach them a few moves. So far the star had remained silent and rigid in the corner, avoiding eye contact and stuffing his face with food. The munchies, Zac suspected, had taken hold.

He also knew that being left alone with these boisterous teenagers would be a much better introduction to the place—and the reason he'd been brought here, rather than being scrutinised by a group of grumpy adults. 'Okay, kids, why don't you take Jaxon over to the gym and teach him the murderball rules?'

'Sure. Then we can whip his...'

Zac cut in. 'Now, now, ladies present. Be gentle with him. Give him a wheelchair too. Play fair.'

One of the boys threw Jaxon a ball, which he caught and passed straight back, rapid fire. 'It's the wrong shape, man.'

'Aww, can't play with a round ball, bro?'

Jaxon grinned. 'Sure I can.' They did a few passes in quick succession.

'We can do more with wheels than you can with legs, man.'

Jaxon caught the ball, twirled it on his finger and finally managed a smile. 'Oh, yeah? We'll see about that. Show me the way.'

Left in peace they helped Tom to clear up. Zac's hands moved cups and plates, but his gaze followed Dani. She wandered across the dining room looking at the many photographs of camps and holidays at the centre filling the walls. When Tom left to answer a phone call Zac went to her side. 'What do you think?'

She bit the corner of her lip and smiled. 'I think you're a very surprising man.'

'I meant about this place.'

'Me too. Bringing Jaxon here was inspired, it's good therapy. The right therapy for him and I'm impressed you saw that. Hopefully he'll learn a few things, like tolerance and patience. And that things are never as bad as they seem.' She peered up at him and beamed. 'I wish I'd learnt that a long time ago. And that being trounced by a bunch of enthusiastic kids who don't have an ounce of self-pity is good for the soul.' She laughed and fixed her hands on her hips. 'So, I have a few questions.'

Her gaze was piercing. He'd never been one to open his heart, so this was rocky ground. 'Fire away.'

'What's your involvement with Treetops?'

'I'm on the board, I help raise funds—that kind of thing.' A vice tightened round his chest. Quarterly meetings were fine, but he hadn't accounted for the rush of emotion being here. In Tom's place. It felt weird. Upside down and inside out. His heart had been torn by Tom's accident and his part in it. But he'd poured everything he had into trying to make things right.

'But why?' Dani looked at him, searching his face. She had a dozen or so questions on her lips and he didn't know where to begin answering them.

'What do you mean?'

'Why here, why Treetops? Why not somewhere else? Cancer research, Arthritis New Zealand, cardiac care? Why *here*?'

'Because it's a special place.'

'I can see that…' Now she put her hand on his arm. 'And who is Tom? And why the weird vibe?'

Damn. That clear blue gaze pierced him. She wouldn't be fobbed off.

He stepped away out of Dani's reach. 'Tom was a friend of mine. He had an accident…' That changed everything.

The reason he couldn't ever commit. Shouldn't. Wouldn't. And latterly the reason he'd chased after his own dreams. He couldn't help the instinctive fisting of his hands, knew his jaw twitched and his voice thickened. He willed his body to relax. 'Treetops is Tom's passion—it also gives him a full-time job and he loves it.' He'd long ago dealt with the pain of the accident, but dealing with the guilt had taken a lot longer. 'We help with the running of it.'

'Who's we?' She meandered along, taking in the pictures, oblivious to the storm raging in his chest.

'Me, Toby—that's Tom's brother—and a bunch of friends who wanted to help.'

'And no one works harder than Zac at raising funds.' Tom greeted them at the door with a tray of steaming mugs. 'Tell Dani about your marathon runs. The ocean swims. The mountain climbs.'

Zac shrugged. It wasn't about the effort, it was about the reward—hard-earned sponsorship that kept Treetops in the black. He owed Tom, owed them all. 'I do what I can—it's nothing, really.'

'It's everything.' Tom put a cup into Dani's hand and directed them both outside towards the gym. 'Zac uses all of his precious and rare spare time to get cash for this place. We have a trust fund which covers most things, but Zac makes the whole place work.' He took a long slug of coffee. Zac wanted to shut his old friend up—making him sound like a saint when he was far from it. But Tom just kept on talking. 'All he ever talked about in med school was being a top sports doctor and rugby, rugby, rugby. Ad nauseum. But he took the safe GP route with a guaranteed income and poured all his time into this. From a distance.' His eyes locked with Zac's and he felt the unspoken disappointment. 'It took heavy pressure from us all to convince him to slow down on the fundraising and follow his own dream.'

Dani watched as Zac turned away, obviously embarrassed. She got the sense that although he loved being the life and soul, he had things so private he didn't ever want them to see the light of day. 'Well, it's great that you can, Zac. Everyone should have a chance to fulfil their dreams.'

And then it occurred to her that Zac needed his job much more than he'd made out. He needed the salary, the promise of more—and he'd need the hefty bonus he'd get if the Jets won. Not for himself, as she'd first believed, but for Treetops. She started to join the dots; his reluctance to protect

Jaxon as there'd be too many other things at stake with his job on the line. His desire to please her father.

She'd been correct all along—he had wanted to impress Daddy Danatello, but for the right reasons, not for Paul's self-serving greedy ones. Too many selfish men had tarnished her ability to judge the good ones.

Tom's brows rose. 'Look, I have a funding application deadline. Do you mind if I leave you two to explore on your own?'

'No worries. We'll be fine, won't we, Dani?' Zac's warm smile reached into her heart and tugged a little. This new light threw up so many more questions. But she couldn't ask him—oh, yeah, she wanted to. Like what had happened to Tom? Why did Zac need to pour everything he had into this place? Why was there a weird static between the two guys? They'd obviously had a deep friendship, but the wounds ran deep.

And she didn't know whether she wanted to probe and get more emotionally invested. The tournament would end and they'd all go back to their separate lives. Little point in allowing herself to get attached to something that would break into tiny pieces leaving her heart bruised.

She followed him into the gym. 'Oh, by the way, what did Matt say when you turned up this morning?'

Zac gave her a conspiratorial smile; out of the glare of Tom's intense gaze he seemed to relax. 'He was fast asleep. So our dirty little secret is safe...'

To her mortification, she giggled, a trait not usually in her repertoire. 'You're making it sound a lot worse than it was.'

'Really? Spending the night with two men isn't your idea of bad?' He made it sound almost exciting. And she had to admit that there were many times when she'd wished it had been just her and Zac in that hot hotel bedroom. 'Jeez, I'd like to see you be really, really wicked.'

Zac's eyes sparkled as they turned to watch the wheel-chair tournament, his voice raised over the loud squeak of tyres on varnish. Jaxon was losing by a long way but the smile he wore told them he didn't care a jot. Dani was impressed; Zac had nailed exactly what the boy had needed. 'He's finally started to loosen up. The fun's in the playing regardless of ability—surely? Hopefully he's learnt a hard lesson.'

Zac wheeled up a spare chair and offered it to her. 'You want to come and play?'

She looked at the concentration and fierce rivalry out there on the court. 'No way. It looks far too dangerous.'

'Chicken.' His mouth hitched up at one corner. 'Girl.'

'Aha. Thank you for noticing.'

'I noticed.' His gaze locked with hers. Heat flickered between them like the beginnings of a smouldering fire that, with one small breath of oxygen, would blaze out of control. All it would take was one step to close the gap between them. Dani hauled in more air; this attraction to him was getting way out of control. So perhaps they should. Take. One. Step. Perhaps one more mind-blowing kiss would erase this need for him.

God, what was she thinking? Of course that couldn't happen. But her feet wouldn't move. However much her brain told her to go, her body craved him.

With what looked like an immense effort his gaze dipped away from her eyes down her body, pausing once at her lips, twice at her breasts. Lower. Her breath hitched. Static jolted through her. Her body hummed with need.

He focused back on her mouth. How could the way he looked at her cause such a riot in her body? The man hadn't even touched her and her nerve endings were on fire. The noise in the room went hazy. Zoned out. All she could hear was the rasp in his breath.

And then his words. 'Watching you sleeping in that red satin thing last night. Man, it was the longest night of my life. I wanted to hold you. Touch you. Make love to you. Way I see it, we have to do something. I'm going mad here. I can't think straight with you around the whole time. All I want to do is kiss you.'

'But...we can't. Not here. Not at the hotel. Not...anywhere.' Her mouth dried.

He inched closer. Her fingers twitched as she held back from pressing her hand against his face. She looked into his dark eyes and connected on a deeper level than she'd ever connected with anyone before. He wanted her. She wanted him. Basic. Feral. Need.

The charge that had run through her in the lift, with his kiss, his damned list, with his body, hadn't dimmed like she'd hoped; it had got hotter and brighter. And she couldn't ignore it any more. 'No. No. This...has got to stop.'

'I know. But I don't want it to.' He turned to look at the game.

The boys were so engrossed they hadn't even noticed there were adults in the room. Let alone adults who were on the verge of carnal.

'Okay.' She swallowed hard and pressed her hand against her chest instead. Felt her tachycardia pounding against her rib cage. Then she turned to watch the full-on game. 'I think Jaxon needs some help.' *So do I.* 'Go and play.'

'I'm gone.' He looked almost relieved as he jumped into the chair and joined the game, laughing and cajoling, and woefully bad at losing, but giving so much of himself effortlessly. He threw the ball to his teammate, who hit it towards goal.

A cheer—no, a *scream*—went up. A gut-wrenching scream of pain echoing off the breeze-block walls.

CHAPTER EIGHT

'QUICK, DANI!' ZAC'S voice dragged her gaze away from the goal to mid-field. 'Over here.'

He was on his knees next to an upturned wheelchair, the wheels still spinning in the eerie silence, a boy sprawled on the floor in obvious pain.

Making her way through the wheelchairs she stopped, glad that Zac hadn't been hurt. Mortified that she cared so much. 'What happened?'

'A spectacular crash and then a tip.'

She crouched next to Zac and helped assess the young lad, who looked about fifteen and seriously unimpressed with finding himself on the floor. 'Hey, are you okay, mate? What's your name?'

'Karl.' His face contorted as he held his wrist.

'Hi, Karl, I'm Dani. Took a real tumble, eh?' She tried to make him feel as comfortable as possible as she pressed along the bones of his arm. A bruise had begun to spread over the back of his hand and blood from a graze spilled onto her knee. 'Sore?'

'Yeah…I seen you before.' He groaned. 'On the telly.'

Oh, no…not the Lady Godiva thing again. 'Aha.' She braced herself ready for the lewd comments. Surely this kid was too young to have paid any attention to the furore over four years ago? But the shame always lingered, hung over her like a shadow. Would it never go away?

'Yep, Dani's with the Jets,' Zac cut in. 'She's the best physio we've ever had.'

'Too right.' Her heart restarted, stalled a little at Zac's affirmation of her skills. But then continued to thump. She didn't need him to fight her battles, to take a piece of her heart when she'd protected it for so long. But this side of Zac—this private, softer side, which made him even more damned masculine—held her spellbound.

She turned her attention back to the crisis. 'Let's have a proper look at this hand. Can you make a fist, Karl?'

His hand flopped in her grip and he shook his head. 'No.'

'Oh.' She watched the boy's face as she slowly pressed along his ulna, looking for signs of distress or wincing at her touch. 'Does it hurt too much to try?'

'No, I just can't make a fist.' He shrugged. 'Paralysed.'

'Oh, gosh, I'm so sorry. I should have thought....' She looked over at Zac for help as heat seeped under her skin. He shook his head. *Don't worry.*

But she did worry. She should have thought, shouldn't have said...

Then Karl's fingers twitched and very slowly his hand fisted.

Big chocolate eyes stared up at her in amazement. The boy smiled. 'Wow. Would you look at that. It's a miracle.'

'What?' Her brain spun into overdrive trying to work out the ramifications. How could a hand suddenly regain movement? Maybe he'd tweaked something in his spine? Brain? Nerves?

Not wanting to freak the boy out she looked over at Zac. Caught them both smiling.

'Quit joking around.' Zac laughed and cuffed the boy's hair. 'She's trying to help.'

'Sorry. Couldn't help it. I'm *para*plegic, not quad. Duff legs, but the arms are okay. Usually.' Karl made a tight fist but winced when Zac touched his wrist. For all his bravado the kid was in pain.

'Great joke, guys. Make it hard for the new girl.'

Next thing she knew Jaxon was at her shoulder. 'Is he okay?' His face had turned ashen white. 'I didn't mean… I'm sorry…I just thought…'

She turned him away from Karl's obviously injured arm. 'Look, mate. It wasn't your fault. This kind of thing happens. Don't worry.'

He spun the wheel of the upturned chair. 'Everything's going wrong. Whatever I try to do…'

'Jaxon, don't take everything to heart. You've just got to relax a bit. Mistakes happen.' His shoulders slumped as he spun the wheel faster and faster.

'It's so unfair.'

'What is?'

'Life.' Was he referring to his own injury or theirs?

'It sure is. And you've just got to man-up and face it. You have an injured foot. You'll be back playing in a couple of weeks. I know this tournament is big for you, but there'll be more games.' She indicated the rest of the boys shooting hoops now at the far end of the court. 'Look at these guys, they have a zillion challenges, but they still want to have fun. You've got to take what you can and make the best of it.' For a young man he seemed to take setbacks very close to heart. 'Karl will dine out on this story for years. How he had a clash with Jaxon Munro. Take the positives before the negatives eat you up.'

She pushed him towards the others. 'Now go and role model some decent staunch behaviour. They rely on people like you to raise them up.' Or was that putting too much pressure on his young shoulders? But it might at least give him something to think about other than himself. When the tournament was done she'd speak to her father about what kind of pastoral care they offered the younger players. What guidance they had for spending their bonuses, saving a bit and taking care of themselves physically and mentally. Something she wished she'd had growing up.

Zac was finishing his assessment when she focused back on him and their other patient. 'Okay, you've got tenderness and swelling here and here. We need to get it checked out thoroughly, find a dressing for that abrasion and an X-ray. We can't be too careful.'

The boy slumped back against his chair, his machismo gone and now his real emotions shining through. 'Great, more broken bones. That'd be just a perfect end to my holiday.'

'Perhaps we could see about getting you a few free tickets to the next game.' Zac winked at Dani and she nodded back. Excellent idea. Zac certainly knew how to deal with the kids. Knew which buttons to press, when to be stern, when to be fun. When to be just straight-up nice. 'I know it won't make up for a fracture, but would it help?'

'Cool as.' Karl's eyes grew wider. 'In the premier box?'

'Don't push your luck.' He play-punched the boy's good shoulder. 'And maybe a few autographs. But first, we have to get you up. On my count. One...two...three...'

In one swift move Zac had the chair upright and Karl sitting in it. 'All sorted. Lead on, Daniella.'

The way he said her name made her stupid legs go weak, as if the world was shifting slightly on its axis. The heat from her earlier embarrassment morphed into a different kind of heat arrowing through her body with lightning speed.

Waking up with him had been divine, spending time here was one step forward to getting him to open up. But even though he'd shared this wonderful place she could see him still holding back—just a little, enough to flash warning bells. Sure, he could do the macho thing, the playboy thing, even the caring thing, but there was still a piece missing. A part of him he kept tucked right away. Something about Tom, about Treetops, made him reticent to share the whole of himself, caused him shadows and pain. Something, Dani sensed, no one would ever be able to completely wipe away from him. Something he didn't even want her to try to do.

'Hey, Dani! Dani! Come in this one? It's way hot. Forty degrees.'

'No, I'm good, thanks.' Dani waved to the group of players relaxing in the largest hot pool. 'Too hot for me, I'm going over there to cool off.'

She made her way to a smaller private pool and laid out her towel. Then stood on the rock border with warm water lapping at her toes as she looked out at the panoramic vista. Serenity was the only appropriate word. The sky stretched pink and orange above her, melting into the views across the still lake out front. Secluded brush stick fencing and giant flax behind gave a sense of privacy and total quiet, save for the gentle trickle of water over pebbles. It was the first time since the tournament began she'd felt peace within her grasp. Maybe, too, it was because Zac had taken Karl for an X-ray—she could get her crazy thoughts together without his disturbing presence.

She closed her eyes and took a long deep breath. *Relax.*

Suddenly she sensed a tremor in the air behind her, a whisper of breath. Felt the heat of his hand on the small of her back. The tiny push. 'Whoop. In we go.'

And there went serenity too. When she surfaced she shook the water from her hair. 'Zachary Price. Typical. What are you doing back so soon?'

'We got fast-tracked. Miss me?'

'No. I was meditating.'

'On what exactly?'

The fastest way to get you out of my system. And definitely not on the way he was looking at her. Or his naked chest. Or the way his eyelashes glinted with tiny droplets. 'Shoulder displacement.'

'Why? It hurts like hell. You planning on doing it sometime soon?'

'Only on you.' She ducked under the water and swam to the far side. Out of view from the others. He followed like she knew he would. Like she...okay, like she hoped. As if by some unspoken agreement.

'This mineralised water should help ease their aching muscles. Supposed to be good for joints too.' If she managed a serious professional conversation she'd stay clear of all the things she wanted to say to him. Knowing more about him was a blessing and a curse. He was more real, more whole. More attractive. She wanted to bypass the emotion, the way laughing with him made her ridiculously happy, the way watching his face light up at something she'd said made her swell with pride. Because if she could bypass the emotion she could get out of this unscathed.

But chances were, she wouldn't.

He sat next to her, his elbows resting behind him on the poolside. 'Maybe it will even soak some of that liquor out of Jaxon. Maybe... Why are we talking about them?'

'Because that's why we're here.' She faltered as she felt his arm extend around her shoulders and draw tiny circles on her skin. Laying her head against him would have been one easy step. But a step too far. 'Not to do this.'

'Dani, it's been a long day and we have another fancy dinner tonight. I've spent hours with kids and drunken athletes, doing X-rays and scans.' He squeezed her shoulder. 'Now I want to spend some time with you. Alone. Is that a crime?'

'Probably. Somewhere.' Certainly what his fingers were making her feel should be illegal. 'Hmmm.'

'That feel good?'

'Yes.'

'Imagine what two hands could do...'

At the sound of voices she wriggled out of his reach. But he captured her leg. She wriggled. He held tight, trapping her against him. Captured. That's how she felt, like he'd ensnared her heart. Like Desere had suggested she do to Zac. Huh, that had spectacularly backfired.

Tutting, she shifted to the seat next to him—it was the only place she could go.

'Hey, move over. Is it cooler in here...?' Joseph and Manu skulked across to the pool. Joseph stopped short of dive-bombing in as he neared. 'Oops. Sorry. Watch out, bro. *Medic meeting.* Out. Of. Bounds.'

'Too right, mate.' With a mischievous glint Zac winked. Out of the corner of her eye Dani noticed his left hand move. He laughed. 'We're discussing your performance, Joe. Try not to peak too early.'

'Hey, the missus has no complaints.' Joseph smacked Zac on the arm.

Irritation rippled through her as she waited until the boys had slipped into another pool. 'Did you just give him the thumbs-up?

'It was more like a twitch.'

'You did. You gave him the *I'm in here* thumbs-up' She shifted to face him. 'What exactly do you talk about in the men's room?'

'Dani. It's nothing. Don't overreact.'

'My father is their boss. I'm trying to create a good impression, not get caught out canoodling in a hot pool.'

'Say that again...ca...what?'

'Canoodling.'

'You are so funny.' He laughed. 'Don't worry. No one knows. Seriously, you think I talk about this? No one cares.'

'I care.'

He stilled. The laughter left his eyes, replaced with something like surprise. As if he'd just worked out the solution to a difficult puzzle. His thumb grazed her cheek and he looked at her face for a second. Two. He smiled and nodded, the one thing she didn't expect from him echoing in his voice—tenderness. 'God help me, Dani. But so do I.'

'So, Doc, did you review Jaxon's ankle again?' Davide leaned heavily on the back of Zac's dining chair and overpowered him with acrid aftershave and a distinct lack of regard for personal space. Danatello's breathing seemed more laboured tonight and a sheen of sweat had formed across his expansive forehead. The pressure of the tournament was obviously getting to the chief as much as those at the coalface.

'Yes. I did have another look and managed to get it scanned this afternoon.' *After dealing with your hungover star, spending the night with your daughter and some seriously sexy talk in the hot pools.* All class-A misdemeanours sure to send Davide's blood pressure skyrocketing. Another reason to keep quiet. 'It's nothing major, but he's still out of the quarter final. He needs to rest it. If we get through to the semis he could be good.'

'If?' Davide's sweaty palm landed on Zac's shoulder. 'When, Doc. When. Can't we inject him with something? The nation's hanging out for this ankle to be fixed.'

'Don't I know it.' Front page news this morning had asked the most burning internationally important question of the day. Not, how to end all war? Or how to solve world poverty? But, will Jaxon play in the final? He was growing to understand Dani's frustration with the celebrity-obsessed media. And with her father. He was growing to understand a lot about Dani. And the more he understood, the more he seemed to like. Realising he cared for her, way more than felt comfortable, was a body blow. He felt like he was sinking and had nothing to grab hold of. Except her. 'There isn't a quick fix, Davide.'

Davide said something and the rest of the dinner guests at the table laughed, but Zac didn't quite hear. From the corner of his eye he glimpsed Dani cross the ballroom. The hairs on the back of his neck prickled, his nerve endings primed on full alert, always aware of where she was and what she was doing. Who she was talking to, who made her laugh, whose arm she had hold of. Like now. As the Samoan coach walked her onto the dance floor.

For a second his gut tightened. He wanted to jump across the table and throw the guy out. Even though the coach's wife was sitting at the next table, smiling and laughing as Dani held the man at arm's length and swirled around in her Jets-red dress. Only, this dress didn't cascade and flow like the smoky-silver one. Falling from tiny straps this one clung to all the right places. And boy, did she have some right places.

He'd seen enough last night to whet his appetite, had barely slept for watching her, aching to place his hand on her shoulder, belly, breast. And now Mr Samoa had his hands on her.

He instantly recognised his tight gut as jealousy. Didn't want that man's hands on those curves, to caress her skin— even if it was just her elbow. Zac wanted to be the one to swing her round to the sultry beat, weave his fingers into that up-do and let the curls fall, run the soft silk through his fingertips, inhale the scent of her organic peppermint shampoo.

Boy, he needed perspective. He couldn't have her. Couldn't ruin both their lives. But he sure wanted her with a fierce rage that he doubted would be assuaged with one more kiss. He sloshed down a glass of sparkling water and tried to refocus on the conversation round the table. But couldn't. Team talk didn't interest him right now.

Which was a damned fool reaction to a woman.

The music ended and she sauntered over towards his table, gave him a coy smile. Perspective be damned, he could easily have a conversation with her without it meaning a whole lot of anything. He grinned back, glad she'd come directly over. But she seemed hell-bent on walking past. 'Hey,' he called to her. 'Can anyone join in?'

She stopped short and leaned into him. 'You can have one dance and one dance only.'

'Just one?'

'You heard the boys in the hot pools—they already think something's going on.' She grimaced and fiddled with one of her straps. 'So any more would look strange.'

'Not when they see how good I am. Or perhaps Mrs Samoa might want to dance with me.' Dumb. Double dumb. Why would Dani care who he danced with?

'I'm sure she would. It's a free-for-all. We're supposed to mingle.' Her lipsticked lips pursed. 'Okay, Mr Light Fantastic, pick a dance. The next one's promised, and then I have one with Mr Sheeran.' In response to his frown she explained, 'Canada. *Chef de mission.* He's about a hundred. Not that it matters.'

It mattered. 'Are we suddenly in 1815? Do you have a card I need to write my name on?'

'Choose a dance, Zac. Make it quick.' She flicked her gaze over to her father, who crooked his finger at her. 'Ching. Ching. Time's up. I have to go.'

Zac's ego slumped as he watched her whisper something to Davide. The old man smiled, then so did she. Haltingly. Then she was up, twirling in her father's arms.

Once again watching her was torture. This time it wasn't because some creep had his hands on her, so much as the way she looked up into her dad's face with so much love and...uncertainty. She didn't smile before he did; she waited to watch his reaction. Then she took her father's lead. Davide patted her back, almost disinterestedly, but she curled into his arm as if she was gripping on to a life raft.

It damned near broke Zac's heart. No one deserved to feel at the beck and call of their parents' affection. Hell, he knew that. That tightening in his gut spread to his shoulders, chest, fists. He wanted to drag her away from this— back to her room, to a different hotel, to a different life that didn't involve sneaking around and stupid rules. To a life that didn't involve depending on his job and paying for a mistake he made a decade ago. Where they could both believe in happy ever afters. No, not a different life, a miracle.

He counted the bars until the end of the song. Waited until her father was back in his seat. Watched her walk across the floor towards Mr Canada...*oh, no, you don't.*

'Zac? What the hell do you think you're doing?' She smiled waveringly at the *chef de mission.* 'I'm so sorry, maybe the next one?' Then she turned her heated gaze to Zac as he wove her out through a back door and into a dimly lit side street. Instinct told him to check for hidden cameras, paparazzi. God, living like this was so claustrophobic. How the hell had she coped her whole life? Simple. She hadn't.

'How dare you treat me like that. You can't just drag me out of a special dinner at your whim, just because I was dancing with someone. Neanderthal.' Her lips formed a tight line, her shoulders shook. God, she was even more damned beautiful when she was angry. But she was right. He'd acted like a dumb caveman. What was happening to him? Dani. Dani was happening to him.

'Why do you do it?' Although he knew the answer. He'd done it so many times himself. Then he'd given up.

'Do what?'

'Why do you pander to him, hoping he's going to take notice? Have you not paid enough for your mistakes?'

'He's my father. I want him to see me for who I am. Not for what I did.' She paced up and down. Took off her shoes and wriggled her toes onto the cemented passageway. Then resumed the pacing. A fire escape loomed above them, metres of metal steps leading to nowhere. The same place this conversation would get him, but he had to try.

'What do you think he sees, Daniella?'

'The daughter who brought shame on his family.' Every single insecurity she had emanated in those few words.

He tugged her to a standstill. 'I see a beautiful woman who has made more than enough amends. And if he can't see that, then he's a damned fool.'

'Like I said. He's my dad. So back off.' The warning in her voice didn't escape him. He was on dodgy ground. If anyone had called his father a fool he'd have rallied too.

'I just hate to sit back and watch you...demean yourself.'

'It's not demeaning. I'm trying to show him I regret what I did. That I'm sorry.' Tears threatened, filled her eyes. She wiped them away. 'Before it's too late.'

'Too late for what? Is he sick? Something wrong with him?' Hell, he knew the answer to that, all right. There was a lot wrong with Davide Danatello.

'Oh, nothing specific. But look at him. He's overweight, breathless, high blood pressure—a heart attack in the making. Any time soon. And I want him to respect me...before he's gone. I'll never forget the look in his eyes when he came to the police station and bailed me out. There was nothing there, no emotion, nothing. It was like I was a problem he didn't even want to acknowledge.'

'How can he not respect you? You're beautiful. Clever. Kind. Everything that he isn't.' Everything he should be walking away from right now. But hell, he couldn't. Not yet. He paused and watched her face soften a little. His grip on her arm relaxed. But he had no intention of letting her go. 'Answer me one question, Dani. Is he worth it?' A question he'd had to ask himself about his own father. He still didn't know the answer.

A solitary tear spilled down her cheek. 'How can you even ask that? Of course he's worth it.'

Before he knew what he was doing, he had both palms cupping her scarlet cheeks and rubbed the tear away with the pad of his thumb. His heart ached to see her cry over a man whose idea of help was throwing money at a situation and turning his back. 'And are you? Come on, Dani. Answer me. Are you worth him? God, I hate to see you so hurt.'

She froze in his hands, stared up at him with sadness and confusion and desire, and he wanted to haul her against the wall. Kiss away her hurt and infuse her with the intense emotion swirling through his veins. He couldn't find a name for them all, but they all started and ended with Dani. He focused on her mouth as she spoke.

'I wasn't worth anything for a while. But yes.' She sighed and nodded. 'Yes. I am worth his respect. Now.'

'So don't ever let him treat you in any way less than you deserve.' He gently pulled her closer. 'Which, by the way, is a lot. You deserve the best. The very best.' Wished with all his heart that he could be the one to give her it.

Then before he could register his actions his mouth covered hers. He heard her small gasp, felt the tiny hesitation and the resignation. Heard the moan at the back of her throat that told him she needed this as much as he did. She curled her arms around his neck, pulled him closer as she opened her mouth, tenderly lapped her tongue against his.

At the touch of her tongue heat fired through him scorching his nerve endings, unleashing a frenzy of need. He tried to hold back, to give her the gentle caress she needed. But his desperation shook through him. He pushed her back against the brick wall, brushed his hand across the bare flesh of her neck, down to the deep swell of her breasts. And she pushed back against him, her hips rubbing against his groin, every moan, every shuddering breath, directing his hands and his kisses.

It was madness, to be kissing her out here in full view of anyone walking past. Madness to start something neither of them could ever continue. Madness, yes, and the most sane thing he'd done in years.

Her palms ran over his shirt, down his back, sending hot arrows of want through him. He clung to her, like a man lost, knowing it was stupid and reckless. But doing it anyway. She dragged the shirt loose, pressed her hands against his back. Skin against skin. Her kisses deeper now, wet and hot. If they didn't stop soon he'd have to have her. And he couldn't. Couldn't offer her anything like what she deserved.

He pulled away gently. Took her hands in his, kissed her knuckles one at a time, then pressed them against his heart. She looked up at him, her lipstick smudged, her lips swollen and eyes muted with heat. Her breathing came hard and ragged. A shoulder strap had slipped down her arm. The hem of the red clinging dress hitched to her thighs, revealing a long leg of pale thigh. Everything about her screamed sex. Bed. Heat. Now. This was killing him. 'Hey, hey. We need to stop this before it's too late.'

'Just because you can kiss like that don't think you are off the hook. That little overprotective act in there could get us both into a lot of trouble.' Her eyes still blazed with passion. Her palm made contact with his ribs, heat suffusing the fabric, searing his skin, his brain.

'I'm already in big enough trouble as it is.' He shrugged away, picked up her shoes, started to head back inside.

She stopped him with a tug on his arm and reached a hand up to his cheek, stroked him softly. 'What the hell, Zac...I'm sick of being nice. Stay here. Stay with me and do a rerun of that kiss. Let's pretend we can do anything we want.'

She wasn't making this easy. A man only had so much willpower. And his was running on empty, and then some. 'No. Let's not. Let's not ruin the good things we've achieved so far.'

'But this is good too.' Her smile wavered. She wiped the back of her hand across her mouth. Reached for a stray lock of hair to wind round her finger.

'Oh, no, you don't.' He put his hand on hers and stopped her reaching her mouth, his thoughts and emotions all jumbled. One minute he was angry, then turned on as all hell, now wanting to help her. There was a name for that. *Certifiable.* But if any good came out of this at all, it would be that he'd stop her hair-eating habit once and for all. 'Okay. Stop. Why the hell do you keep doing that?'

'It takes my mind off things. I've had a lot of disappointments.' Her voice was thick, sultry and filled with desire. She rubbed her hip against his thigh. 'Like right now. Starting things and not finishing them...'

'Gee, and a fur ball would really help with the seduction process.' He kissed each fingertip. 'You're good and strong, princess. You do not need to do it. Again. Ever. Or I'll get some scissors and chop it all off... Try making a fur ball with a pixie crop.'

'You wouldn't dare...' The corner of her mouth curled into a half-smile.

'Don't tempt me.' He wrapped the loose lock behind her ear. Resisted temptation to fist her hair into a bundle and lose himself in it. 'Don't tempt me with anything. You hear. Stop that.'

She was now running her thumb along the inside of his thigh. 'You like it?'

'You have to ask?' He stepped sideways. 'Look, we have to go back inside. Be grown-ups and talk politely to the nice international guests.'

'Stuff them. I don't want to talk to anyone else. I want to do this. With you. Here.' Dani tried to control the need shivering through her. The way he looked at her with such reluctant desire snagged her heart. The guy was struggling as much as she was. 'You might think you're being chival-rous, but it's just annoying. You can have me. Right now.'

Okay. Great. She'd handed herself to him on a plate. If he was shocked he didn't look it; in fact, a smile spread across his face. But she'd shocked herself. She'd never been so bold and brazen. But then Zac wasn't like anyone she'd ever met. And even though she knew as much as he did that neither of them could do more than hot kisses and possibly hot sex— definitely hot sex—but after that? She didn't have any kind of plan past *I want you*.

She ached for him in places she hadn't ached before. And that ache was putting paid to any sense left in her numb brain. Did she trust him with her heart? They were a long way from that. Probably not worth risking everything on. She was scared to give him too much of herself in case he took it and destroyed her. Scared to meet him even a quarter of the way. Scared to death that she'd get way too lost in him.

But right now none of that mattered. All her body craved was his touch, his mouth on hers, him inside her.

'That's a lot to offer a guy.' He relaxed his hold on her hands. For a second she wondered if she'd scared him off. Turned him off. But the warmth in his eyes radiated as he looked into her eyes. He looked the most aroused she'd ever seen him. Felt the most aroused too. 'And what do you want from me?'

'Lots of things.' Too many. Right now sex was top of the list. But it ran way deeper than that, who was she trying to kid? 'Friendship. Fun. I'm so tired of denying myself things.' Why couldn't life be easy sometimes? 'Just give me one thing, Zac. Then I won't ask for anything else.'

'Anything, princess. Except sex. Although it kills me to say it. You know we can't do that. However much we want to. And I do. Believe me. I have done since the first second I saw you.' His finger stroked her cheek and a lump settled in the back of her throat. Any other man would have had her there in the side street.

Then he frowned. 'Dani, I can't give you anything more than a good time. You have to know that. Please don't even ask.'

The lump in her throat seemed to grow thicker and bigger. Even though she knew he was right, and was being more honest than he needed to be, it was hard to hear.

'There are parts of you I want to get to know so much, Zac. But I think they're the parts you don't want to share, right?' The shadows in his eyes. The crack in his voice at Treetops. She ached to smooth them all away, in the same way he'd tried to help her. But he'd put a barrier round them, and there was no way he was going to let her penetrate it.

His eyes shuttered down a little. 'I'm sorry. I can't. I won't make you any promises.'

'Because of Tom?'

'Tom.' Again the shadows.

But that was the closest he'd come to admitting he was holding back and why. One step closer. Two steps back. 'Okay, so no promises. But you didn't say anything about wishes.'

He laughed but his eyebrows knotted and wisps of shadows still remained. 'Wishes? What is this? Cinderella?' His shoulders flexed back and his playful smile slowly returned. 'Okay. I reckon I can do Prince Charming.'

'Too right. That would suit you down to a T. Tomorrow is our last free day before the chaos starts. I want to spend it with you. One day. Doing normal things that normal people do. Not work.' She watched him step back. Not physically, but he took some distance. She needed to bridge that gap. The hell with being tentative or shy. She needed, for once in her life, to ask for something. 'Not celebrity stuff. Not rugby stuff. Some fun. Just one day to pretend I can have a normal life, with a normal man.'

'Hey.' He stepped back for real this time and glanced down at his über-sexy penguin suit. 'Less of the normal.'

She laughed. 'You have way too high an opinion of yourself.'

'I was always taught to speak the truth.'

'Okay, then.' She rolled her eyes. 'Give me one normal day with an *exceptional* man.'

'What about your father and his bunch of crazy rules?'

'Stuff him too. Why is everything always about Davide? Today he had a game of golf followed by a Thai massage. In contrast we spent our day off babysitting a bunch of juveniles after a sleepless night.' At the memory of Zac's bare legs entwined with hers she couldn't help but lean into him again. Stroked his jacket lapel through her fingers. Breathed him in. *Stroking. Kissing. Biting.* 'I don't see why we can't play too. Nobody's going to know, or care. I just want one day. And I want the whole damned fairytale.'

'You, Daniella, live in an upside-down world. To everyone else, with your rich and famous celebrity family, you are the ultimate fairytale.' Reluctance warred with desire in his eyes. He scrubbed a hand over his chin. 'But I have things I need to do tomorrow. Phone calls to make. I thought I'd talk

with the Fijian doctor, see how he's going. He's been struggling to find an orthopod in Hamilton. And—'

'Hush. You work too hard.'

'And now you know why it's so important.'

Knowing it made her want him more. His passion for
Treetops fired a different kind of passion in her. 'Other
things are important too. Relaxation. Fun. You can't spend
all your time keeping everyone at arm's length and burrow-
ing yourself in work and fundraising. That's not a life.' She
tugged on his lapel. Was his reluctance just a fob-off? Had
she totally misread him? But no—his kiss wasn't a fob-off.

She didn't trust her reactions to him. Couldn't work out
if he was searching for reasons not to spend any more time
with her. And after seeing his closed reaction to Tom, she
didn't know if she was chasing a dream that he just wouldn't
participate in. But while her body hummed and buzzed
around him, and her brain had programmed itself on this
one-man mission, there was little she could do to stop. One
day would be enough to satisfy her cravings for him. Surely.

Would it? Or would she spend the rest of her life looking
for this one thing she would never be able to have again?

'Come on, Zac.' She stepped closer, watched the heat in
his eyes. Felt his desire for her. He definitely wanted her.
His body told her what he wouldn't say in words. 'You know
this is getting way out of hand. This kissing, dragging me
off the dance floor. The heat in this alleyway is scorching.
We need to deal with it and move on. Neither of us wants
commitment. We both know where we stand.' Her forth-
rightness surprised even her. 'I just can't work out what else
to do. This morning was fun, but who knows if we'd last
a whole day without the added bonus of a hungover chap-
eron?' She wriggled against him. 'Hell, ignoring it doesn't
seem to be helping. And it's certainly not helping you any.'

'That obvious, huh?' His eyes fluttered closed for a second as he struggled with whatever demons he had in that mixed-up head of his. 'And after? What do you want from me?'

'There can't be an after, we both know that. We go back to being colleagues. Workmates. The team. Focus on winning the tournament.' She held out her hand. 'No ties. No commitment. Just a whole lot of fun. One day. Are you in?'

'I guess one day off won't kill me. I have no idea how we're going to do this without creating a stir. Or making things worse between us.' He took her hand but instead of shaking on the deal he pulled her close and whispered into her ear, 'Okay, princess, your wish is my command.'

CHAPTER NINE

Operation Fairytale
Rendezvous time: 10:15 a.m.
Rendezvous point: Basement car park, lot no. 245
Dress code: Casual. Hat essential.

NEXT MORNING DANIELLA picked up the piece of paper that had been pushed under her hotel room door, read it for the fiftieth time and laughed again. A wild buzz rushed through her. Crazy. Stupid. Reckless, even for one day. But just the thought of seeing him had her fizzing.

That Zac hadn't turned her down was one thing. That he'd gone as far as to take her so seriously was another level altogether. Could it be possible to be satisfied with a few snatched hours? She didn't know, but she had to try. Then she could put the whole weird crush thing out of her mind.

Or was she out of her mind already? Could one day ever be enough?

Her heart did a staccato dance as she reached the basement car park. Through the gloom three suits walked past her. None gave her a second glance. Clearly the disguise worked. She just needed to make her wobbly legs cross to lot 245 to reach Zac and...

'A campervan?' She laughed as he ushered her inside the souped-up shiny oldmobile. Still unsure of the direction their relationship was headed she watched him for clues. But he gave nothing away. 'I've always wanted one of these, it's so cute. Like a little house. You could go anywhere, be anyone, in one of these.'

'It has a cooker, sink and fridge. And a bed.' Squishing down on a pristine gold-and-blue bed his smile transformed from warm to hot. So that's where they were headed. At least in his mind anyway. At her playful frown he grinned. 'Could be useful for something?'

'Sleeping probably.' She raised her eyebrows but enjoyed the flash of daring in his eyes. 'It's seriously gorgeous. But honestly? Bright yellow? I thought we were trying not to attract attention.'

'A slice of sunshine the hire company told me.' He patted the ancient dashboard lovingly, then took his seat and cranked the engine. He wore a hippy-chic trilby, dipped over his forehead to almost touch dark shades. A faded black T-shirt hugged his toned frame and straight-leg black jeans wrapped his long legs. Something about his dark clothes and the sneaking around gave the whole escapade a dangerous edge. And that pushed a zillion sex factor buttons. 'It's VW vintage, lovingly restored. And, if you'll care to take a look, it has tinted windows so no one will see you.' He smiled proudly as he reversed out of the space. 'You said normal. What's more normal in these parts than a tourist? Oh, and we need to hurry.'

'Why?'

'You'll see. Now just duck down a little as we swing past these idiots.' The crowd of photographers camped outside the hotel entrance immediately turned at the sound of the van's throaty engine. But as soon as they saw the vehicle the paparazzi turned focus back to the main hotel doors with ill-disguised disappointment. Her heart slowed a little as they drove past without the slightest recognition.

'Perfect.' Zac grinned and ran his gaze over her. 'Great disguise by the way. With that monstrosity no one would ever think you were a celebrity.'

'How dare you insult my favourite sweatshirt? I love it.' She looked down at the hoodie she'd hurriedly bought from the hotel shop. I Heart Rotorua, it said in cheerful pink embroidery, complete with a cluster of weird-looking rainbow-coloured sheep. That, with her cheap navy baseball cap and dark sunglasses, screamed anything but designer wardrobe. And definitely not Danatello. But Zac's pupils flared when he looked at her and heat radiated through her. 'Yes. You're right, it is hideous. But it's all I've got, so you'll have to put up with it.'

'You could always take it off.' He looked at her with wicked intent. 'And I could always help.'

'Whoa. Early days, Zac. It's going to be a long day.' But a shiver of excitement wove down her spine as if one touch, one look, from him would have her burning up. This outing was such an excellent idea—burn up the lust. Then get on with the rest of her life. 'Keep your eyes on the road.'

'So does that mean no? Or just not yet?'

'It means I have an even worse T-shirt on underneath that says *don't go getting any ideas*.'

'Oh, I've got ideas. Some great ideas.' He grinned, his profile highlighting his strong cheekbones and proud jawline. She fought an urge to run her finger along that jaw. Down his throat. To that little dip where his pulse flickered. Then all the way down that T-shirt to...

His voice lowered. 'But you didn't answer my question. I need a little guidance here. Was that a no? Or not yet?'

It was a *soon*. But they hadn't set any rules for the day and she sure as hell didn't know much past her crazy irregular heartbeat and intense fizzing. 'Zachary Price, you are getting way ahead of yourself. You must have been a woe-fully precocious child.'

'I was very advanced in many areas.'

It occurred to her that she didn't know much about his past at all—other than some curious experience with Tom that he refused to share, and that his parents were lauded academics. Eschewing all rationality she planned to find out more later. Discover what had made him the way he was. It was just a matter of finding the right moment. This wasn't it. Pushing him too early would have him hotfooting it back to the hotel. 'So you excelled in Seduction class? Gee. I hear there's a very low bar. Especially for doctors who know how to lay on the charm.'

He laughed. 'They had to introduce a whole new level just for me.'

'What? Advanced Overconfidence and Wishful Think-ing?'

He steered the van round a sharp corner, and grinned. 'No, honey, Satisfaction Guaranteed.'

'Ha. Yeah right. Keep right on driving.'

Out from the cluttered buildings in the township a wide blue sky opened up either side of the road. Rolling hills and fields stretched out in front. The Rotorua sulphur smell thinned as fresh air flooded through the open windows.

For the first time in a long time her chest felt lighter, she didn't look behind her or worry about what the gossip ma-chine was saying. She felt free. Free from her ordered, con-trolled life. Even though she had great girlfriends she never usually spent so much as an hour with a man. Certainly not one she was attracted to.

Clasping her hands together in her lap she peered through the window. 'So where are we going?'

'A magical mystery tour. Just sit back and enjoy the ride. Not too far now.' He pressed a fingertip to her lips. The temptation to kiss it, suck it right into her mouth, almost drove her wild. But all too soon he gripped the heavy steering wheel with both hands and turned into a popular tourist attraction. 'First stop. Agroworld.'

'Really? This is it?' Whatever she had in mind it wasn't this. A bunch of sheep and cows in paddocks.

'Hey…this is just the beginning. Wait and see.' Judging by his bright smile he was pretty excited. And he appeared to have put a lot of thought into it—the cute yellow van, this place. His attention to detail struck a resonant chord. No one ever put a lot of thought into her—unless it was to rip her off or sell her out. 'Ever milked a cow? Fed a lamb? Want to get down and dirty?'

Thought you'd never ask. 'When would I do something like that?'

'Thought maybe your sister might have pulled you along when she did that reality farm show.'

'No way. I was deep in the Inner Sanctum. Sure, she suggested I visit, along with a million camera crews. As if I'd have gone. Why would I? She never bothered to come and see me. None of them did.' The back of her throat burnt at the memory. A whole month and not a single visit. '"Deanna's Dairyfarm Diary," what were they thinking?'

'Money probably.'

'And more fame. Always the fame.'

His thumb ran small circles over her palm; she focused on that, trying to ease the ache in her chest. The gentle stroking mesmerised and soothed her. When his fingertips ran up and down her forearm her heart beat in sporadic jumps. A tingle of awareness shuddered through her, catching her breath.

She angled her head to look at his face, daring to see what message shone in his eyes. And there it was. I want *you.* Not the fame. Not the Danatello fairytale. Not just sex. But her.

For a few seconds she allowed herself to believe he'd have

been her rock when she was sick. He'd have visited. He'd have been faithful and kind. Thoughtful. He wouldn't have dumped her and sold his story.

She dropped his hand. It was pointless to think like that. He hadn't been there. He wouldn't be there if she ever needed someone again. Not the way she wanted someone to be there for her.

He'd promised her one day. That was all he could give. So this was it. Better make the best of it.

Zac's heart pinched at the sudden transformation of Dani's face. Where she'd been relaxed and bright a couple of seconds before her frown told him they'd veered into difficult territory.

That damned family, caring more about a facile reality TV programme than Dani's life had obviously hurt.

And he obviously cared more than he wanted, if the knot in his chest was anything to go by. Hell, the more time he spent with Dani, the more she edged a little deeper into places he didn't want her to go. It was getting more and more difficult to keep up those barriers.

Time to make things light. He checked his watch, then started to count. 'Five, four, three, two…bingo. Right on time.'

The frown lifted. 'What are you doing?'

'A student tourist bus is just pulling in. I thought we could blend into the group.' He nodded towards a large intercity *fun bus* across the car park. Streams of camera-laden youths disgorged, jabbering in foreign languages.

'And you knew they were coming…how?'

'I rang to see when the busy times would be. They told me a student tour arrives every day at ten-thirty. So to avoid this time if necessary. I thought it would be perfect.'

'It is.' She squeezed her hand on his knee, sending his synapses snapping and a swift rush of blood to his groin.

For a second he thought about abandoning the whole day's project and making love to her right there. But that wasn't what this was about. This was about showing her a good time, a special time. The other stuff could wait.

Could it? Whoa. This was definitely dodgy ground and then some.

A couple of hours later, after the farm tour, a sheepdog show and some intense sheep shearing, he joined Dani up on stage to feed greedy lambs. Watching the animals mill around, fighting to get to the milk, reminded him of the ruck and maul of the paparazzi.

Her eyes widened as she laughed. 'They're pulling so hard at the teat I can hardly hold the bottle. Look at this one, he's so cute. Oops...wow, he's strong.'

'Come here. Let me help.' Zac sat in close behind, his legs straddling her, and wrapped his arms over her shoulders. Sure, it was corny as hell trying to find an excuse to sit close. But her smile had tugged so hard at his heart that he just needed to touch her. To remind himself that this was real and time was short.

'This is so much fun.' She turned her face up to him, her breath grazing the side of his neck. The lambs made little bleating sounds that made her chuckle and that tickled his skin. He rested his head against hers and took the punch of pride that resonated through his chest at her smile.

'Well, there's lots more to come. So when you've finished with little Lamb Chops there, we've got a lunch date.'

'Lamb chops indeed.' She gave him a stern look and covered the sheep's ears. 'Hush. You'll scare him.' Then she nuzzled the wiry fleece. 'He didn't mean it. Nasty old Zachary.'

His heart snagged again as he watched her stroke the animals and wave goodbye to little Lamb Chops as if the darned thing was her pet. Taking his offered hand she jumped down from the stage. Kept tight hold as they ran across the car park back to the van.

'That was great.' She smiled up at him before climbing in. 'Thanks.'

'My pleasure.' God knew, he meant it too. 'Now, let's go eat.'

'You are joking?' Ten minutes later her voice was thick with laughter as he came out of the fish and chip shop with a hot bundle of paper that smelled like salt and vinegar heaven.

'Got to have a good old-fashioned Kiwi lunch.' He drove as fast as he dared down to the lake shoreline. Pulled up in a little deserted car park off the main drag and set up a picnic table and chairs outside in the weak early-autumn sunshine. Dappled light glinted off the serene deep blue lake that bordered the town and then stretched out across to dips and troughs of volcanic hills, some covered in the deep lush green of grass, others peppered in pine forest or majestic flax.

A family of ducks waddled past their feet, clearly in a hurry to finish some pressing business at the lake edge. Nothing else stirred.

Grabbing a couple of champagne glasses and a bottle of fizz from the fridge Zac smiled at Dani's frown. 'Don't worry—I only break some of Davide's rules. It's just sparkling grape juice. Nothing but the best for my...' His words stalled. His what exactly? His girl. His friend. His date? 'To one day.'

'One day.' She seemed to hesitate slightly, took the glass and sipped. Then dipped the hot chips in tomato sauce and ate with her fingers. Whilst she'd opened her heart to him yesterday he got the feeling she still didn't quite trust him. To be so wary and on her guard the whole time, never knowing who was a true friend, had to be hard. But her smile seemed genuine. 'These are so yummy. You know how to treat a girl.'

'I certainly do. Sunshine and hot chips beats a swanky restaurant any day. Tell me, Daniella, what do you do when you're not touring the country with a rugby team? I don't feel like I know much about you.'

'And yet you know so much more than most.' She reached across and squeezed his hand. 'But I'll do you a deal. A question for a question.'

Not where he wanted to be going. But he weighed up the pros and cons. If he wanted more information he had to give some too. Fair deal. She had a point. 'Okay. One question each. And then we'll see how we go.'

She nodded, took a breath. 'I love my job at St Clare's. It's in a poor area so there's lots of need. The girls are often stuck in a situation at home that they don't know how to get away from.' Her shoulders lifted. 'I know what that feels like. For them sport is a good way out. So I work hard to keep them well and active. When I first started there I got a bit of resistance from the staff and parents. But I proved my worth, the girls seem to like me and not one of them has ever mentioned where I am or what I do to the press.'

'I admire you. It would take a lot of guts to give up what you knew to work somewhere like that. You have your own place? A flatshare?'

'That's two more questions, Zachary. I'm counting.' She winked at him, easy and assured. The shadows that seemed to dog her earlier had fled. When she talked about her real life—not the crazy of now—her eyes lit up. 'I have my own cottage which I love with a passion, and a small garden. I can do what I like. No pets though. But now I'm seriously thinking about getting a lamb.'

'Oh, sure. That's the perfect pet to have in suburbia. No

more lawnmowing required. And no more plants. Period.'
She didn't need a pet, she needed someone to love. Someone
to love her back. 'It was hard growing up in the spotlight,
I imagine. With all that madness around you.' He held up
his palm. 'Okay. Yes. I'm trying to make it into a statement
not a question. Give me a break here.'

She grinned back, but fiddled with her fingers. One mention of family and she tightened up. But for once she didn't
do that hair fiddly thing that drove him crazy. 'It felt like
my parents were only interested in our novelty value. What
better than a cute baby-shaped accessory to carry around on
your hip? Deanna and Desere were beautiful and compli-
ant. They love the attention too. But I just hate being talked
about, scrutinised. And was never good enough.'

'The hell with that. You're better than them all.'

'Not how I felt growing up. It was like there was something wrong with me. Like I didn't belong in that family,
somehow I'd got there by mistake. They didn't want me to
be me, were always trying to mould me into something else.
I was never a Danatello.'

A weight pressed against Zac's chest as familiar anxiet-
ies rolled over him. 'Your father deserves to know how that
kind of treatment feels.'

She paused, obviously deciding how much to tell him.
'You've got to understand—he grew up poor and was badly
abused by his dad. Beaten and hurt. Granddad didn't just
want him to be someone else, he physically tried to make
him into something else. Harder. Colder. And some of it
rubbed off. Now Davide continually needs to prove himself.'

Zac hauled in oxygen. However badly Rufus had treated
him over the years, it hadn't been that extreme and he'd
never resorted to physical abuse. 'When you put it like that
I can see why Davide's like he is. But it's no excuse to make
you feel so unloved.'

'There's always a reason behind everyone's actions, Zac. Even people like my dad.' She reached across the table and fixed him with a thoughtful gaze. 'Now it's my turn to ask. I have how many questions? I'm starting to lose count.'

'Why am I suddenly nervous?' He glanced at his watch. Phase two was fast approaching. And he needed an excuse. Quick. 'Actually, we need to go.'

'So this is it? You clam up before I even get one question? That is so unfair.' As she followed him to the main body of the van, he practically felt the frustration emanating from her. The familiar rush of guilt washed over him. Yeah, he needed to open up. But he didn't want to spoil her day.

'Why don't we talk while we're driving?'

She slammed the table and chairs into the cupboard. 'Because you'll be evasive.'

'Who? Me? Evasive?' He poked her in the ribs. A tickle, really, but enough to make her squirm. 'When?'

'Unfair again, Zachary. Trying to attack a defenceless maiden.' She poked him back, once, twice. Giggled. Pushed him. He lurched against the sink, lost his footing and pulled her with him. Squarely onto the bed.

'Hey.' Dani wriggled upright, still cross with him. He'd wedged more space between them, something she'd watched him do time after time, something he'd become an expert at, and she didn't know how to bridge the gap. Apart from giving him time. And she didn't have that. The guy had issues and clearly didn't want to share them with her. It took two, right? So she should just up and leave. If only tangling with him wasn't fast becoming one of her favourite activities. 'So how do we get out of this?'

His fingers tiptoed along her spine. He flashed a wicked smile and pulled her gently towards him. The corners of his mouth kicked up and his voice lowered. 'Do we even need to try?'

'Yes. Is there any point in this? You won't give me any part of yourself. You won't talk. And apparently we're...'

In a hurry.

But the taste of his mouth on hers stopped the words. Stopped the thoughts. His hand palmed the back of her neck as he pulled her close. She relaxed into his kiss, his heat and scent enveloping her. She fit into his space, entwined her legs around his, pressed her hands around his neck.

Unlike the passionate heat of last night this kiss was slow and tender, soothing. Nurturing. He took his time, running his tongue along the line of her lips, the edge of her teeth, cupped her face in his hands. The exquisite softness of his touch was torment and pleasure in equal measure. She felt his hands tremble as he held her, his ragged breathing. He kissed her eyelids, the tip of her nose. Softly, so divinely softly, it made her heart soar.

Exhaling a shuddery breath she clung to him, unwilling to let go, unable to move her hands from his fisted shirt in case the spell broke. Her body hummed with desire, building and building, burning for his hands to find her most sensitive places. Aching for him to fill her and satiate this ever-growing need for him. But still he held her face, stroked her cheek as if they had all the time in the world. As if they had the whole of for ever.

Then he kissed a trail over her cheek, down to her neck, to the dip of her shoulder. She arched against him, every cell in her body strained for his lips. He slipped a hand under her sweatshirt, brushed feather fingertips across her back, to the sensitive skin at the side of her breast. After slowly unclipping her bra his hand finally found her nipple. Stroked it, tweaked. Sucked it into his mouth, driving her wild with need.

'You are the most beautiful woman I've ever met. The most amazing.' His voice was hoarse and thick as he dragged his mouth from her skin. Tugging her sweatshirt over her head he grinned. 'And this has got to go. I've been wanting to take it off all morning.' His grin broadened as he stared at her rose-coloured silk camisole. 'You lied. It's not a T-shirt at all.'

'Oops. I had to say something to stop you. Or we would never have left the damned car park.'

'If I'd known what was underneath I'd have made sure we never left.' Flicking first her camisole, then bra to the floor he dipped his head and licked her nipple again, the sweet heat of his tongue making her shiver. First one breast, then the other, he sucked and stroked, sending ripples of pleasure through her. Then found her mouth again.

His need for her was obvious and she pushed against his hardness. His eyes sought hers and he smiled with a look so tender tears sprang at the backs of her eyes.

Never had she felt so cherished, so beautiful. So wanted. This was what she'd dreamt of, what was possible, what was always out of reach. And now she'd finally grasped it she didn't ever want it to end.

Everything he said with that look was mirrored in her heart. She ached for him, not just physically, but longed for him to fill the empty hours of her life, the gaping hole she pretended she'd filled with other things. To wake up with him every morning, to be the last thing she saw at night. To share the laughter, the tears and everything in between.

She pulled him to her, covered his mouth with hers and told him in that kiss how much of herself she wanted to give. How much more of him she craved. She ran her hands down his back, felt the rough curve of his spine, the soft smooth skin, the dip in the small of his back. Felt him shiver as she ran her fingers along the top of his jeans. And, like a sharp jolt of static, his kiss deepened, his breathing intensified.

All Zac knew was that he was lost with need. This beautiful, sensuous woman who stoked such intense heat within him was in his arms. And the desire to be inside her almost overwhelmed him. Whatever was right or wrong, for one day or for ever he couldn't fathom. Right now he wanted to make love to her. Long, slow, hard, fast. Again and again. She filled him with a fierce longing like he'd never had before.

He eased off her jeans, always aware of her fingers floating around his zipper. All it would take was one small loss of control and he could be filling her. But he had to take this slow. This was her day.

She moaned against him, spurring him on as his fingers travelled across her belly, down the inside of her thigh. Her fingers fisted his T-shirt when he pulled her panties off. And the cry she gave as he slid a finger inside her almost melted his resolve.

'I want you, Zac.' Her voice was like a purr against his chest as she bucked against his hand. With his thumb against her hard nub he brought her to a frenzy. Her hands gripped his shirt tighter as she contracted around him, pulling him in further.

'Not yet.' He managed to somehow stop her releasing his zip. Kept his own wants wrapped up as he gave her again and again what her body craved. 'This is for you, first.'

'So don't stop. I need you.' Her eyes fluttered closed as he slid his finger in again.

I need you too. Goddamn. He did. He just didn't want to admit how much. And now he wouldn't stop for anything. 'Open your eyes. I want to watch you.'

'Oh, Zac.' She wrapped her legs around his, squeezing his hand against her, and writhed against him. Her gaze never left his. Those deep blue eyes glittered with wonder and passion. The honesty making him want to hold on to her and never let go. Never had he felt this kind of connection, two halves making something so complete. Even without sex he could make love to her, give her what she needed. Hell, what he needed.

Then he kissed her again. Her mouth was hot and wet as she cried out and shuddered, closing her eyes as release took her.

Watching pleasure shake through her body gave him a powerful punch somewhere near his heart. In his heart. It wasn't just her unleashed sensuality. It was more than that. A whole lot more. Something he didn't want to admit. He'd spent years avoiding this kind of intimacy. But she'd drawn him in, beguiling him, entrancing him, until he couldn't deny it any longer. He'd let himself get more deeply involved than ever before. He wanted to protect her. To make her smile. To watch the light in her eyes shine, because of him. Bottom line, he wanted to make her happy.

For a long moment his heart thundered against his ribs. What the hell to do? He had nothing to offer her except for this day. After that he had work to do. Work. Work. Always work. That had become his refuge and his cross to bear. Dani deserved a life of love, not an absent lover who put his career first.

He looked back at her, her blonde curls spilling over the cushions, her smile calm and serene, oblivious to the torrent of weird emotions crashing through his chest. And so she would be, because hiding his emotions was something he could do.

When her eyes opened again her smile turned from serene to hungry. 'That was so good. You have magic hands.' Her fingers crept to his zipper, which still strained under the force of his erection. His body told him what his brain was trying to eradicate. *Whatever you may try to believe, matey boy, you want her with every damned fibre.*

'You are amazing. Wow.' He stroked the flat plane of her belly.

Her pupils widened. 'Your turn now.'

'I can wait.' One thing he knew, he couldn't have her here. And if she unzipped him and took him in her hands he'd lose all control. Some vague rationality seeped into his brain. He edged away a fraction and smiled. He had another seventeen hours with her and intended to make every one count, not lose control now and have her regretting what they'd done. He wanted a perfect day to store in his memory banks for ever. 'I'm loving this, princess. But we need to go. There are other things I have planned.'

'No…don't stop.' It was more moan than words as Dani ran her palm over the tight muscles in his shoulders and pulled him closer. She couldn't let this end here. Couldn't bear the thought of not being in his arms again. Soon. 'Please, Zac.'

He pointed to the steamed-up windows behind chequered curtains. 'You deserve better than a quickie in a campervan. Seriously, we need to stop.'

'I don't care. I love this campervan—it's like a little house. Our house. No one can get to us in here. Outside is another land. That's all pretend and crazy. In here is real. I like our kind of real.' And it was then she realised she'd been so terribly wrong. One day with Zac could never be enough. She wanted him in her life tomorrow and the next day…. 'I want you to make love to me, Zac. Now.'

'And I want to, more than anything I've ever wanted in my life.' He raked a hand over his hair and shrugged. 'But not like this, hiding out, breaking rules. Besides, we don't have any condoms.'

'You have two thousand damned condoms.' She laughed

and patted his back jeans pocket. Taking another opportunity to feel his butt in her hands and pull him just a little bit closer. 'Are you sure you don't have any there?'

He shook his head. 'I didn't want to be tempted, so I left them at the hotel.'

'You did what? Typical. Bring them when we don't need them. Don't bring them when we do.' She gave herself up to the laughter and anger and all the muddled-up emotions swimming through her veins. Kissed his chin and wriggled against him. He was starting to loosen up, give something of himself.

One day.

Best. Day. Ever. 'You have to stop trying to save me. I know the risks. And the silly rules.' She tiptoed her fingers down to the top of his jeans and gasped at the heat and hardness still there. 'But there are lots of other things we can do instead. I'm a grown woman and you...' Licking his cheek, moving down to his neck where he squirmed against her, she moaned again at the same time he did, then ran her fingers down the straining zip seam of his jeans. 'You...are a very grown man.'

'God, princess. No.' His smile belied his words, but his hand covered hers and moved it away. He held her fist against his heart. 'I have a timetable to stick to. So please...' This time his kiss was hungry and fast. And it was even harder when he pulled away. He let out a grunt, half moan, half laughter. 'Please. Stop.'

'Trouble is...' A sigh escaped her lips as the harsh reality sank in. Despite all her efforts to protect herself, she was falling for him, hard. She laid her head against his chest, listened to the raging thunder of his heart and felt her own heart beat in perfect sync. 'I don't think I can.'

CHAPTER TEN

'OKAY, YOUR TURN…what else can we add to the list?'

'Daniella, it's impossible to drive a lumpy old van safely and think about these kinds of things.' But Zac grinned as his mind whirled with images of Dani and a whole lot of trouble. 'Chocolate mousse?'

'Oh, God…' She leaned in, her flowery scent driving him mad with desire, and nibbled on his ear. 'Just stop the damned van. Now. Look! There's a motel… Oh. You passed it?'

'I told you, we have a lot more surprises in store. And all night.'

'All night?'

'One day, you said. Last time I looked that was twenty-four hours. Of which a good ten are at night. We could do a lot with chocolate mousse in that time.' He pulled the van into a lay-by and took her into his arms again. After the longest, sweetest kiss so far he dragged himself apart from her. If he wasn't careful one day with Dani could rapidly turn into one week. One year. One lifetime.

Whoa. Steady. He couldn't lose focus. On the Jets winning. On the trust. On what happened after the madness.

But images of Dani in her smoky-grey dress, the heated kiss after dinner, the light in her eyes with Lamb Chops, with him. The way she'd refused to let Jaxon be punished for a mistake…the way she felt in his arms as if she was meant to be there. Everything about her mesmerised him, made him ache for more. Forget the yellow campervan, Dani was fast becoming a slice of sunshine in his dark life and he was in danger of being dazzled. 'At this rate we'll never be able to tick the things off my list.'

'But I prefer the other list.' She snaked her fingers down towards his zipper.

'Oh, God, I've created a monster.' He couldn't help smiling. 'But we have a—'

'Yeah, yeah. Your blessed timetable.' She snatched her hand away and planted another kiss on his cheek. 'God, I just love that dimple. Okay, drive on McSexy.'

As Zac turned the van up the Treetops driveway a weird prickling at the back of his neck chased the desire from his veins. Something didn't feel right. A large menacing black car with heavily tinted windows sat bang in the middle of the car park. Too executive, too fancy, for a kids care centre. Like the godfather had come to tea. His stomach knotted. Surely not.

'Why are we coming here again?' Dani's grip on his knee tightened as they neared the house. 'Is this part of the surprise?'

I wish. 'I'm dropping off those tickets we promised Karl for the game tomorrow. Then you and I are supposed to be going horse-riding. I arranged with Tom that we could use the centre's horses.'

'Hoping for a Lady Godiva rerun?'

'Well…now you come to mention it…really, more like a ride into the woods.' As he saw Davide, then Matt, and then Jaxon step out of the sedan wearing dusky frowns he knew that plan was over. As was the rest of Dani's special day. It didn't look exactly like a welcoming party. His heart thumped strong and fast. 'But right now I think we might be headed to hell.'

He cranked the handbrake and turned to Dani. Gone was the cheeky smile and the light in her eyes, replaced with dark shadows and a grim taut line for a mouth. 'Hey, it might not be bad.'

'Oh, yeah? Just look at Davide, all puffed up like a damned blowfish. It's bad, all right.'

'Davide, Matt, Jaxon.' He nodded to each in turn. 'Fancy seeing you all. How did you know we'd be here?'

'Jaxon suggested you might be.' Matt stepped forward; his breathing seemed laboured today. Unusual for him. His cheeks were unnaturally red and he stooped slightly. Probably the stress of Davide and the tournament getting to him. After the chaos was over there needed to be stress management talks and decent strategies put in place. 'We needed to speak to you urgently, but neither of you answered your phones. Jaxon eventually told us about this place.'

'Why? What's the problem?' Dani's voice shook along with her hands.

Couldn't this wait? And why the hell did this strong beautiful woman crumble every time she looked at her father? It drove him insane. 'My phone never rang, must have been out of range. And just what is the problem that you needed to speak to us on our day off? We are allowed some time out and privacy.'

'You want privacy? Then stay out of the headlines.' Matt pulled a newspaper out of the car and squashed it into Zac's outstretched hand. The look on the coach's face told him everything he needed to know. There would be no *after the tournament*, no winning, no bonus—not for Zac anyway. A vice tightened around his chest. He had a sense of everything slipping away, out of reach. This day. His job. Daniella.

Everything he'd worked so hard towards—gone. In a moment of weakness when he'd made the wrong choice. Again.

'No...' He shook the paper and looked at the pictures of Jaxon staggering into the bar, waving his arms wildly and demanding alcohol. Of Dani and Zac carrying him out. Grainy CCTV images, but clear enough to see that the country's great rugby hope had been drunk and disorderly, with two accomplices to clear up the mess. All the while C.J. had stood in the shadows, watching, calculating, a towel in his hand, relentlessly cleaning glasses. No point in explaining, it was all there. 'You just can't trust anyone, eh?'

'Well, he made big bucks selling his story.' Matt sneered. 'And ruined our reputations in the process. The media's having a field day.'

The paper crumpled in Zac's tight fist. 'Wait till I get hold of him.'

'Leave it. He'll be long gone.' Dani's hand covered his wrist and she shook her head. 'They always are.'

It was as if she'd expected the betrayal. Her face was almost as red as Matt's, eyes brimming with tears, but she smiled and shrugged. How could she take it so calmly? Her acceptance almost tore his heart to shreds.

That fierce protective streak she brought out in him fought its way to the surface. Whatever happened he had to convince her father that she had nothing to do with any of this. He wouldn't stand by and watch her get hurt again. No point her losing her job or Davide's respect when she'd worked so hard to get it back. She was a damned good physio; she'd see the team through to the final. On her own if she had to.

He glared at Matt, then at Davide, screwed the paper into a ball and threw it onto the plush leather car seat. 'Yes, Jaxon made an error of judgement. And I may have done too, in hiding this from you. But Dani had absolutely nothing to do with this.'

'But…it was…' She stepped forward, her fingers hovering over her mouth.

Zac closed her down with a slight raise of his hand. 'I made an executive professional decision. Alone. Jaxon was suffering from an acute setback. His mind wasn't focused on the implications of his actions. As his doctor I assessed him and believed it was a temporary lapse. I wholeheartedly believe he won't do it again.' He looked towards Jaxon, who stared blankly at the ground. 'And I know he's very sorry.'

'Not good enough.' Davide spat his words out, anger shimmering through his body. 'I won't tolerate people going behind my back. Jaxon belongs to the Jets. To the nation. He's in *my* team. I should have been told.'

'No. Absolutely not. Break my code of conduct for you? No way.' But he'd sold his soul to the devil when he'd signed his contract. All medical matters had to be discussed with management. He searched for Dani's gaze, the fire in her eyes gave him added strength. Yes, they'd trodden difficult ground, but ultimately they had done the right thing. And, in the end, that was all that mattered. He could still hold his head high professionally; he'd just need to find another job. If only there was one that he'd want as much as he'd wanted this. 'Talking broken bones is one thing, but acute stress is entirely different. I knew we could work it out, given time. And we had plenty of that before the next game. He's my patient and is entitled to confidentiality.'

'Not at the cost of the rest of the team. We have rules.' Davide's finger waved in Zac's face. 'You broke them and dragged my daughter down with you.'

'No!' Dani stepped forward again.

'Leave her out of it.' He fought back the anger surging through him. 'I have professional standards to abide by. And common sense to adhere to. Your petty rules only serve for you to laud power over everyone, Davide. But they don't work so well for the rest of us. Give the boy a break, everyone makes mistakes. Even you, when you left your daughter high and dry and desperate for help.'

'How dare you. You don't know anything about what happened then.' Davide's hand dropped to his side.

Zac opened his mouth to speak, to rally back at the old man, but Dani's hand was on his arm. 'No. Leave it please.'

'Oh.' Matt's gasp had them all turning to the car. His grip on the door had his knuckles turning white. His shoulders slumped forward, his head dipped.

Knowing he wouldn't want any fuss Zac turned him away from the staring group. 'Are you okay?'

'I could do without all this. I'm fine.' Matt nodded, gasped. And again. 'Darned indigestion. Won't go away.'

'Let's go sit down.' Zac started to peel Matt's fingers from the door. But the coach wouldn't budge. Held on to the metal for grim life. 'I'm not having a discussion about this, Matt. We need to go inside, or go back to the hotel. And you need to rest up.'

'The hotel…is a zoo of hacks…braying for the…story.' Matt's breathing had worsened. He seemed to be sucking in air as fast as he could. With a trembling hand he rubbed his chest. 'The media…want Jaxon's blood. Mine… Yours.'

'Are you sure you're okay?' Zac grabbed Matt's wrist and took his pulse. Too fast. 'Dani. Quick. Matt's not well. I think he's going to…' As Matt slumped into his arms Zac steadied himself and took his friend's weight. Dani ran over and helped lower him to the ground. She loosened Matt's tie as Zac made as quick an assessment as he could. Conscious. Tachycardic. Tachypnoeic. He ran his hand over their patient's sticky forehead. He was burning up. 'Where's the pain, mate?'

'Here. Man…make it stop.' Matt curled into the pain and rubbed his right side.

After a few seconds he seemed capable of speaking again. Zac continued with his questioning. 'Sharp? Dull? Cramping?'

'All the bloody time. Sharp.'

Right-sided upper abdominal pain. Not cardiac. Zac blew out a breath. Good. A heart attack out here in the middle of nowhere would not be good news. He glanced over to Dani; she looked up at him with such trusting eyes—but with a flare of defiance in there too. She was probably fuming over his refusal to allow her to take any blame for the Jaxon fiasco. The way he'd talked over her, which he'd never normally do, but under the circumstances… And right now he wanted to slap a kiss on those hungry-looking lips. But he had work to do. Always, always work came first. 'Is the pain radiating anywhere?'

'Back. Shoulder.' Matt tried to sit up, winced and lay back down again. 'But…game tomorrow…'

'Let's worry about tomorrow, tomorrow. Do you feel sick at all? Have you been sick?' Or was that on the list of Davide's stupid rules too? No showing any kind of weakness. Zac examined Matt's eyes. Very slight yellowing of the sclera. 'Have you had the pain for long?'

'On and off….a few days. Didn't want to say anything.'

As he'd surmised. 'Okay. We have to get you to the hospital. I think you might have gallbladder inflammation. Possibly gallstones. But it could be a lot of things. You need an ultrasound, X-ray and a whole screed of blood tests first.'

Davide finally joined them after watching the events unfold from a distance. He looked shaken and frail, and if it wasn't for the fact this man held his future in his thick livery hands Zac might have felt a stab of pity for him. His team was falling apart in the middle of his most important effort at garnering success. And his daughter was at the centre of controversy, again. That had to hurt.

Her shaky smile bit him to the core. He wanted to wrap his arms round her and take her away from all of this. Now her day was spoilt, and depending on her father's whim, her immediate future too.

Take control. This time—*this time*—he had to make the right choice. Not put himself first. Follow his heart, not his head. And this meant choosing for her.

They both knew his job was over. He needed to pick himself up and walk away, not drag her down with him, as Davide had so eloquently put it.

If he distanced himself from her now, made a clean break of it, then her mission to make things better with Davide could begin again. She'd get the respect she'd been seeking for years. Maybe the chance to bask in her father's favour. 'Dani, why don't you drive your father and Jaxon back to the hotel in the campervan? Try to get some rest before to-morrow. It's going to be a big day. I'll take Matt to hospital in the car.'

'Wouldn't an ambulance be quicker?'

'No.' He forced himself to look away. The sooner he left, the better. He'd head straight home to Auckland once he got Matt settled. He focused again on his patient, forced all emotions to the back of his mind. Ignored the sharp stab of pain in his heart. The day was shot to hell. His life was shot to hell too. 'It'll take too long for an ambulance to get out here and then back into town. Can you phone ahead to the hospital and let them know to expect us?' He helped Matt into the back seat, made him as comfortable as he could. 'I'll see if Tom has any pain relief I can give you. Are you okay with that, mate?'

Matt waved weakly. 'Sure.'

Dani nodded, drew Zac to one side. Okay, so the emotions hadn't been quite pushed as far back as he'd hoped. Just looking at her made his heart hurt. Knowing he'd probably never be this physically close to her again rocked him to the core. But he resisted the temptation to touch her.

She smiled a hopeful smile, haunted and anxious. 'Let me know how you get on. Call me.'

'Okay.'

'And…?'

'And. Nothing. I guess. Day over.' He shrugged. Hating himself for coming across so cold. But the mask he'd worn for ten years had slipped and he was fitting it on again for size. He didn't want to hurt her or himself. But if that was the price they had to pay to save themselves, then he'd pay it. They needed to end everything now.

Dani bit her bottom lip. Swallowed deeply. Took a huge breath and blew slowly out. Steadying herself, he guessed. She knew as well as he did that this was not the time and place to say goodbye. But she also had to know things couldn't possibly work out between them. Never could have. 'Okay, you take the car, that'll be faster and smoother for Matt. And I'll…' She hauled in another breath. Her lip wobbled. 'I'll drive the campervan. Talk later?'

He leaned close. 'I'm sorry, Dani.'

She nodded. Wiped a tear before it ran down her cheek.

'But…' Davide interrupted, oblivious to his daughter's heartache. Again. His mouth opened. Closed. Opened again. 'I can't go in that thing.'

'Davide, get in the van.' Zac could barely contain his anger.

'I can handle this.' Dani stopped him, took the keys from his outstretched hand. She turned to face her father, dark clouds whipping behind her eyes. And Zac glimpsed a steel he'd never seen from her before. The same steel, he guessed, she'd used to conquer her demons. The same steel she'd use to get over this fling, this day...whatever it was they'd had. 'Daddy. Get in the damned campervan.'

Davide gaped and flustered. His cheeks reddened further. 'But...'

'To hell with your image. Arriving in a bright yellow campervan might not be your idea of a good PR campaign...' Zac could have sworn he saw a flicker of amusement in her face now. But it disappeared as she glared at her father. 'It's an emergency, so suck it up and put yourself further down the pecking order.'

'But...'

This time her shoulders snapped back and she looked her father square in the eyes. The strong woman Zac had always known was there finally blossoming in front of her father. 'For God's sake. It's not always about you. The man's ill. For once in your life, show some sympathy. Have a bloody heart.'

CHAPTER ELEVEN

'Zac, are you back yet? What's happening with Matt?'

What's happening with us? Dani threw her cell phone onto the hotel bed. 'Answer your phone!'

He'd been gone hours and hadn't responded to any of her texts. All through the contretemps with her father she'd watched as he'd carefully withdrawn. Bit by bit he'd distanced himself, until there wasn't a hint of warmth in those dark eyes any longer. He'd become the ultimate detached doctor. The heat of their frivolous chatter and long kisses had faded into nothing and there'd been nothing she could do about it.

Guilt bit deep. Guilt and a whole lot of something she didn't want to put a name to. She'd stood by and let him do it. Didn't fight for him. Or for the decisions they'd made about Jaxon. She'd let Zac take the blame for something she'd begged him to do. No one had ever protected her like that, taken the blame for something she'd done. Normally she was the first thing they'd trample over in order to get closer to her father. But Zac had put everything on the line for her.

And he'd fired back at her father too. Given her the courage to do the same. But then he'd edged further away, almost as if he'd made a conscious effort to do so. Fought for her, but not for himself and definitely for any kind of notion of *them*.

Her brain whirred with confused emotions. The fizz of

their kisses, his tender touch, the sexy chatter, the crushing realisation that C.J. had sold them out. And now the reality that Zac would leave and she would stay and there was nothing she could do about it.

A weight pressed in her chest, heavy and dark and tight. She fought for a breath, tried to steady the nerves pinging through her body like a crazy pinball machine. It was over. Could never be real no matter how much she'd wanted it to be. She'd endured a lot in her life, but nothing had prepared her for how much she'd fall for him, or how much she'd hurt when things spiralled out of control. She felt like she was clinging to crumbling rock as everything collapsed around her.

As she picked up the phone again frustration rushed through her. Where the hell was he? He could be anywhere. The hospital. The other side of the world by now. Or the other side of the wall. She'd rung his room too many times to count, had listened to the phone ringing off the hook through the elaborately patterned wallpaper.

Zac? We need to talk.

More silence.

The romcom movie on the TV was driving her mad with its *love conquers all* message. The lovers wedded and bedded. The soundtrack, some soppy tune filled with sloppy sentiment, brought brief tears to her eyes. But nothing was ever like in the movies, with the assured happy ending and eternal belief in love. For a balmy few hours she'd allowed herself to believe in the dream, but in reality it had never had a chance.

Zac! Answer me!

Flicking the mute button on the TV she crawled onto her bed and craned her neck at the adjoining door to his room. Listened hard. Sure enough his message ringtone beeped.

Anger mingled with the frustration into a hard knot in her gut. He'd been there how long?

Busted! You are next door. So ANSWER me.

Again the message tone. She tapped her fingertips on the cell phone keypad, waiting for him to answer. Felt the vibration before her own ringtone sang.

Matt's in surgery. Gall bladder. He'll be fine but out for the tournament.

She contemplated throwing the phone across the room. But at least he'd answered. Cold and impersonal, and not what she'd hoped for, but better than nothing.

Is that it? I don't get an apology?

She could have sworn she heard him curse. Although it may have been a door slamming further down the corridor.

Apology for what?

Being pig-headed and trying to save me. AGAIN!

A hard rapping made her jump. She hurtled across the room and swung the door open. 'Zac?'

He leaned against the doorjamb, arms folded across his chest, muted frustration blazing in his eyes. 'Next time you can damned well save yourself, woman.'

Next time? Everything about his stance, from his blazing eyes, the curled lip, the space he kept between them, told her he didn't intend staying. 'So I've been demoted from princess to woman, now?'

'Personally I think it's more like a promotion. You've

earned your stripes. But take it how you want.' Now he leaned closer, the scent that had been taunting her all day wafted round her. She wanted to grasp it, savour it, bottle it so she could take it out in the dark moments and keep him close.

'And can you stop with the texting already? I'm trying to sleep. It's been a hell of a day.' The forced jollity in his voice zapped her strength.

'I was starting to get concerned when you didn't answer. It is normally a common courtesy to reply to a text.' She yanked the door wider in an effort to entice him in, but he didn't move. 'So everything's okay?'

'Yep. Matt will be fine. You evened things out with Davide?'

'Not really. He barely spoke to me the whole way back. One step forward, two steps back.' She shrugged, forcing the ache in her throat to ease. So they were talking about everyone else, but not about them or where they were headed, or what they felt.

Hell, Zac was a master at avoiding that. He was a master at a lot of things. Being funny, tender, giving her what she needed, everything she asked for. Except himself. She swallowed hard. 'Daddy didn't take kindly to the laughter when we drove into the hotel. But he put up a brave fight. Told them he'd been treating me to a dad-daughter day out.'

'That man sure can spin.' His shoulders relaxed a little. He gave her a small smile. 'I'm glad things are working out for you.'

'I didn't say that, we've a long way to go. Thank you for what you did, but you didn't have to take the rap for me. Dealing with Jaxon like that was my idea all along and I'll make that clear to Davide. I can fight my own battles.'

'No point us both being out of a job. You've got a lot more at stake.'

'Really? Davide versus Treetops. You win hands down.'

'Well, it's done now. So don't argue.' His chin jutted up. 'As long as you're okay, I should go.'

No. Was there any point in laying out her feelings to him? Would he treasure her words or throw them back in her face? The girl who'd asked for a day but wanted for ever. She didn't want to take that risk. 'Okay. Go.'

But he didn't move. Silence stretched between them. He just kept looking at her and she looked straight back at him. Not really at his features—although they were intensely gorgeous—but the way he reached deep into her soul, the way he made her feel. The sheer beauty of the man. Heart and soul. There was so much she wanted to say to him but she didn't know how. Didn't want to turn their fling into something it wasn't.

He shrugged. 'Yeah. Okay. It's late. Been a long day.'

She tried for light. 'I don't know why you're standing here anyway, knocking on my door at this hour.'

'Because I knew I'd get no peace unless… Oh, hell.' He marched into the room and closed the door. For a moment she thought he was going to crush her against his chest and kiss her, but he brushed past, gripped the back of the chaise longue and stared out the window into the darkness. 'Unless I said goodbye. Before I go.'

That was when her heart began to break.

He swiveled to face her. Dredging every bit of strength he could to say what he had to say. But the vulnerability in her eyes pierced his soul. He'd crashed in here wanting to purge himself, but what would that do to her? Why should he burden her with his past? With the reason he was walking out of here. Why should he tell her his true feelings? That he probably loved her. If that could be possible after such a short time. Certainly, he could grow to love her. Fall deeper. Harder.

Hell. Yes. The overwhelming need to protect her, to be with her, to touch her, all made sense now.

He hadn't seen that coming and now the reality smacked him in the stomach like a low hard tackle.

He loved her.

Could it happen so quickly? So out of the blue. He'd been hiding from this kind of thing for so long he hadn't seen the warning signs.

He loved her and there wasn't a damned thing he could do about it except walk away. He was too coward, too driven. Too messed up by the mistakes and choices he'd made. Too tarnished by regret, by the knowledge that love and a career like his couldn't exist hand in hand. The only blueprint he had was his parents' sad existence and he couldn't force that on anyone, least of all on Dani.

Dani, who he'd had no business falling in love with. Dani, who had fought a very public battle and come out stronger than anyone he'd ever met. Dani, who could have the pick of a million better men.

The ache in his stomach spread to his chest. Just seeing the uncertainty in her eyes made him know he was doing the right thing by walking away. He didn't ever want to see her look like that again.

'Sit down. Talk to me.' She pulled him to the chaise, pushed a glass of apple juice into his hand. Sat opposite, trying her hardest to look disimpassioned, and failing badly. He could read her now, knew her brave attempts to rise above her emotions. Knew she was hurting as badly as he was. He controlled the wild beat of his heart and the urge to haul her into his arms. If he kept an emotional distance, didn't tell her how much he'd fallen for her, how much he loved her, it would be easier to let her go. 'Before you go where, Zac? Where are you going?'

'Back to Auckland first thing tomorrow. But I've made a few calls and there's a job coming up in Melbourne.'

'Wow. Melbourne. That's a long way.' Her eyes widened, glistened. 'You don't waste time.'

'I can't afford to be out of a job.' He forced juice down his dry throat, then put the glass on the coffee table between them. 'Australia's a big place, there are a lot of opportunities.'

'And what about the opportunities here? I could talk to Davide.' The hope in her voice almost broke him. 'If you want… We could tell him about us. I could try to persuade him to keep you on…for my sake.'

He avoided her gaze. How much would she give up for him? Don't. *Don't do that. I don't deserve it.* 'I would never let you do that. Besides, it's too late. I've resigned. Before Davide could sack me. It looks better on the CV that way.'

'Oh sure.' She slammed her fist onto the table, stood and stalked across the room. And then back to face him, her hands stuck on her hips. 'Of course. The CV. I was right about you all along. Career comes first.'

'It's who I am. What I am. A doctor first. I never made you any promises.'

'No, you didn't. But hell, Zac, there's more to your existence than work. What about a future? A family? A life?'

He reached for her, took her hand and pulled her to sit close. One last time. Was it only a few days ago they'd laughed on this couch? He'd barely slept for wanting to take her, be inside her. Be with her. What kind of a future could he give her? Not one he'd choose for a wife. And if that was where this conversation was heading—marriage and kids— he had to end it now before she got any more crazy ideas. Before he started to believe her. 'Work is my life.'

'Then too damned right it's selfish. It's all about you. There's no room for compromise. Or is it just an excuse because you can't commit to anyone but you?'

'It's a reality. I need to get money for the trust if not for anything else.' He forced a smile. 'The marathons are killing me. I need to give my legs a break.'

'So you martyr yourself...' She paused. Frowned. Twisted to face him, her eyes huge and bleak. And he waited for the inevitable. The one thing he knew he couldn't avoid any longer. She looked at him, expecting him to be honest. 'What the hell happened, Zac?'

His throat clogged with guilt and anger. Faced with telling her the bare facts he let his cocky mask slip. 'I let Tom down when he needed me.'

'I can't believe that. How? You were there during his accident?'

'No. That's the point. I wasn't.' He dragged in oxygen, tried to shift the rock blocking his throat. But it didn't work. He forced his words out. 'I met him on my first day at school, we clicked straight away. He was like the brother I never had. We went on to med school together—always ultracompetitive at everything, either he came first or I did. If he won something I made sure he didn't win it a second time. At med school I used to rib him that he had it easy—his parents paid—but I'd already fallen out with my parents over who they wanted me to be.'

'I hear ya.'

'But you have a chance to make things up with Davide. Take it.' He smiled. They both had PhDs in dysfunction, but she would win Davide over. How could she not? 'They pegged me to be a geologist like them, to work for their foundation. The *family firm* they called it. Which was a joke in the first place. We're not a family. We're a group of people who happen to be connected by bloodline.'

Stroking his hand she laughed. 'You want to play *who's got the most dysfunctional family*? Thinking I might win.'

'Probably.' The smile came from deep in his heart. They'd both had enough drama to last them a lifetime. 'In the end I told them to stuff their bloody rocks. Paid my own way through med school. I wanted to show them. But just passing wasn't good enough. I am my father's son after all. I needed to be the best. I pushed myself. Worked hard. Played hard.'

She fired back at him. 'There's nothing wrong with wanting to be the best, but not to the detriment of a full life.'

'Yeah, and that's what me and Tom thought. We had a blast. Until the final year. Exam time. His course work had been poor, he'd dropped a few grades.' Now the pressure in his chest started to push in, stopped his breath. But he'd shared so much more than he'd ever actually spoken out loud to anyone else. 'He started acting a bit weird. Stayed in his room a lot. Wouldn't come out to the bar. Stopped looking after himself. To be honest I lost focus on him a bit. My exams were so important to me, I had to pass. To show my parents. And I had to beat him.'

She frowned. 'But that was just the same as normal, right?'

He couldn't sit still any more, had to get up—get some space. Shift the tension in his body. He let her hand go and stood. 'Looking back, he was acting far from normal. One day we were offered the chance to scrub in on a surgery. He said he didn't want to, he was going home. And I was kind of glad—thought the extra hours with a surgeon would give me an edge. Just before Tom left he looked me in the eye and said, "Goodbye, Zac." I was too hyped up about the surgery to notice his words. But later…after…I realised his intention. By then it was too late.'

'What did he do?' She covered her mouth with her hand, swallowed deeply. He watched the movement of her throat, the gentle softening of her features. Thought how easy it would be to melt into her arms and try to forget. But he couldn't, wouldn't ever forget, used Tom's accident as a reminder of who he was. A doctor, first and last. Nothing more.

'Drove his car into a wall. At high speed.' It seemed so long ago and yet the hurt in his chest was fresh. Or was that the hurt of now? He didn't know. A dark chasm opened up in his solar plexus. He'd lost the Tom he knew and now he was walking away from Dani.

She stood too, leaned against him and rubbed her palm up and down his back, her voice filled with concern and warmth. 'Zac, I'm so sorry. But you must know it wasn't your fault.'

'How can you know that? How can I?'

Dani shook her head. Her mouth slanted into a thin line. 'He did that to himself. He needed help.'

'And I should have seen that but I was too focused on winning. Everything changed then. Our friendship, everything. I was so angry. Couldn't forgive him for what he'd done. Couldn't forgive myself for not being there.' Still couldn't. No matter how many marathons or mountains climbed. Couldn't even bear to visit Treetops, a reminder of what Tom had become, in that damned chair. And of how much he'd lost. 'The police said it was an accident, but I *know*. I know it wasn't. What scares me is that I was so damned focused on my work I missed his symptoms—or chose not to look too hard.'

'You mustn't beat yourself up about this. The man seems fine now.'

'You think?' He turned to face her. 'In a wheelchair?'

'I mean, he seems really together. And you...well, actually, there was a tension between you. But you could do something about that if you wanted. Make it right between you. Talk to him, like this.'

'I can't. I've avoided anything deep with him for years. When I heard about Treetops and what he was trying to set up I jumped at the chance to help, but I don't have any contact with him except for quarterly meetings. It's not the same. We're not mates.'

'You could be again.' Her eyes held a glimmer of hope he wanted to cling on to. 'And so, what does all this mean for us?'

'If I can choose not to save my friend what other dumb choices will I make in the pursuit of my dream job? Clearly I have a hard time sorting out my priorities between work and the people I care for. That day, I was assisting in theatre and we saved a kid's life—I chose that instead of Tom. Medicine isn't just a day job, something you get up and do and then forget. It's about life and death and you carry it with you. I don't ever want to be in a situation where I have to choose like that again. I don't think I could.'

'For goodness sake, Zac, it doesn't have to be like that. Thousands of doctors marry and have happy family lives.'

'When I was growing up I promised I'd give any kids I had a better experience than mine. Parents who were around. Who *noticed* you. To take this Jets job I had to give up a practice I'd spent years building, leave behind friends and family. Cut ties and take a risk on income while I retrained. But I was more than happy to do it. Broke apart everything I knew to rebuild. What would I choose to sacrifice with a wife and kids? Birthday parties? Schooling? First steps? It's not going to happen.'

As he said these words everything became clear to him—he'd spent his life trying to prove himself, but what had happened with Tom had knocked him sideways and veered him from his path. With the Jets he'd found it again, and needed to finally be who he wanted to be. Despite Davide, he'd find a way. Without the encumbrance of a family or a girlfriend.

Dani had been a delicious distraction but he had to let her go for both their sakes. She'd never know just how deeply he'd fallen or how hard it was to walk away. 'And I'd be chasing the limelight. A high-profile job means high media interest. Interviews, cameras, invasion of privacy. I wouldn't want to put anyone through that kind of pressure if they didn't want it.'

'But...'

'No, Dani.' He put a finger to her lips, so tempting to let her convince him. To pretend they could make it work. 'Don't ever put yourself at the bottom of anyone's pecking order. You deserve to be cherished and loved and left in peace to live a happy life. Every single day.'

'I could live with every other day.' Her wobbly smile made his heart crumble into pieces.

He tore himself away from her. Stretched his arms, filled his lungs. Needed to breathe fresh air, to think. To plan. To gather the strength to walk. Needed to work out how he'd survive the next few days, weeks, without her. But he would. Hollow, perhaps. But still breathing.

'So that's it?' Dani watched the shadows flit behind his eyes and knew she'd lost him to all the excuses he could find to keep his distance. After everything he'd been through who was she to deprive him of chasing his dream? Even if it meant a life without her.

Now she understood what made him the man he was, determined and ambitious, loyal and hardworking, but she knew beyond that he had the capacity to love, to have fun, to give. To be whole. He just didn't trust himself. Didn't believe he could have everything.

And she knew there was absolutely no chance of changing his mind. He might be leaving tomorrow, but in reality, he'd already gone.

And hell. He'd never made her any promises; in fact, he'd been adamant to make her understand there would be no commitment. He'd never mentioned love, or even fondness. Maybe she was just another sticker on his Pretty Boy star chart. Desere had been wrong. Enticing him and encouraging him to stay didn't work. He'd made up his mind, and she just wasn't enough to keep him here.

'So I'm left here to win this tournament while you go swanning around in Melbourne?' She forced the smile, forced the brightness in her voice, forced the pieces of her heart to hold together a few more minutes. 'And now Matt's out too. So much for teamwork.'

'The assistant coach will step up and I'm sure Davide will find another doctor. He might have one up his sleeve right now.' He'd reached the door, his shoulders slumped. He was going. Going. 'Only, promise me one thing.'

'Yes?' She made it across the room, breathing him in one last time.

'It's a big ask.'

'What?'

He tipped her chin. 'You won't even think about having sex-free sex with him too.'

'How could you say such a thing? Never.' Reaching his cheek she ran her finger over his dimple. 'I only have sex-free sex with really special guys.'

'Excellent.' Then his mouth covered hers and she held on to him, stifled the sob erupting from her chest, controlled the shaking of her shoulders. He didn't need a simpering fool in his arms. She found her self-control.

He finally dragged his mouth away, nuzzled his face in her hair. 'You'll do a fine job, Dani, and have a wonderful time in Wellington with your school and your cottage and little Lamb Chops, or whoever you decide to share your life with. But if you need anything just let me know. I'll be there.'

I need you to stay. I need your kisses like oxygen. I need to wake up to your smile. 'Oh, sure. The playboy in shining armour. I'll be fine. Like I said, I don't need saving.'

'I mean it. Anything at all. Let me know.'

And then he was gone. The door closed, leaving her staring at the bare wood.

She wanted to chase him, shake him, show him how loving could be, what was possible. But he'd hardened his heart and made up his mind that it couldn't work—that even though he'd tried hard to save her, he didn't have it in him to save them both.

And, in a way, he was right, he wanted the exact kind of life she'd spent years shunning. She just hadn't expected his leaving to hurt so much.

So, for the third time since she'd met him she leaned back against the door, hugged her arms around her chest and groaned. Only this time she finally let fall the tears she'd held in since the moment he'd stormed into the room.

She'd never believed in love at first sight, or wanted happy ever afters.

Until Zac.

Damn him.

Somehow, from the second he'd grabbed her arm in front of that room of hacks, he'd grabbed her heart too. Squeezed and squeezed until she'd been incapable of fighting him any longer. Shook her long-held beliefs, turned her reality upside down. The way her body responded to his touch, the way he made her laugh, the way he kept trying to save her, as if it was his, and only his, job to do so.

The only man who had seen the real her and cherished it. Irritated the hell out of her, but made her heart ache too.

And now what?

She couldn't imagine another day without him. Didn't want to wake up tomorrow and not be a part of his complicated messy life.

She loved him. There it was.

Her hand cupped her mouth, held in her gasp. All her attempts at protecting herself had come to this? She was more exposed and raw than she'd ever been. She loved him and had done since the moment she saw him.

This was so far from her plan it was laughable. She wasn't supposed to fall for him. A fling. A day. That's all she'd wanted.

But she'd got a whole lot more than she'd bargained for. Love. It was as simple and as impossible as that. She loved him and there was nothing she could do about it. Except let him go.

CHAPTER TWELVE

Jets in Chaos for Title Chase

To lose one member of the management team may be regarded as misfortune. To lose two seems like carelessness.

It doesn't take a genius to realise that changing the management team in the middle of the year's most important tournament is folly. But Davide Danatello has a garish lack of regard for genius. Hence his swift dismissal of top sports doctor Zachary Price and temporary sidelining of world number-one first five, Jaxon Munro. What happened behind closed doors in Rotorua will long remain a mystery. We can only surmise it had something to do with the tacky photographs of drunken behaviour covered up by the medical team, but exposed by valiant News reporter, Frank Weston. Luckily they still have talented physio Daniella Danatello as the glue to the Jets entourage. Unshaken by the speedy exit of Zac Price, the man they once called her lover, she has single-handedly kept the Jets on track through a squalid quarter final and a desperate semi. Without her magic hands spreading stardust over the team's escalating injury tally the country's hopes would have been dashed. We can only hope those healing hands, her skilled physiotherapy and Jaxon's return for tonight's final brings the victory Danatello has been promising us...meanwhile, the nation holds it breath.

NO PRESSURE, THEN, DANI. Zac threw the newspaper onto the pub table and sipped his pint. The cloying taste stuck in his throat and did nothing to assuage his thirst. For two weeks restlessness had eaten away at him. Throughout flights and interviews he'd gone through the motions, given stock answers, left his heart out of any decision-making. After all, his heart had let him down too much already. A huge aching chasm had opened up in his chest and nothing—not even today's final—could fill it.

Sure, he knew the only thing that would help was Dani. But he couldn't do that to her. She'd blossomed in the past two weeks. He'd watched her confidence grow with each televised match—the only chance of seeing her—refusing to take his eyes off the screen for a second in case he missed a brief shot of her. Her take-charge attitude on the pitch-side had dragged the team into this final. She'd clearly managed to put her private life in some corner and focused on her professional responsibility. Which was a damned sight more than he'd managed to do.

He patted the ticket in his jacket pocket. One hour to go. All around him people dressed head-to-toe in red were singing and chanting. The Jets, the team he'd followed his whole life, whose players he thought of as friends, whose woes he'd lived and breathed since before he could speak, were going to bring home the cup. And the excitement, emanating from every fan, from every corner of the now scarlet city, failed to register behind his thudding heart.

All eyes were glued to the pub TV where the screen showed the Jets backroom staff giving the warm-up messages and final checks in the changing room. Zac craned his neck and scanned for Dani. There she was. His heart kicked a little. Okay, kicked a lot. She was tiny in comparison to the players, but her charisma and competence shone through. A grin for Manu. A nod to the new coach. A hand on Jaxon's shoulder. Even a brief smile for her father, who in turn smiled back at her. She looked relieved, relaxed. In control.

Zac closed his eyes. Walking away had been the right thing to do. It had.

'Thanks for the ticket, mate. I really appreciate it.' Tom drained his glass. 'Now drink up, or we're going to be late. I want to soak up the atmosphere in the stadium. It's not every day we have a victory like this to celebrate.'

'No worries.' As he stood to clear a space through the busy bar for Tom's chair, Zac paused. The past couple of weeks had also seen baby steps in getting their friendship on track, no more hiding behind work, or fundraising. He was paying back. Make it right, Dani had said. He took his seat again. Making it right involved words not just actions.

'Tom. You know…what happened…back then.' He was no good at this. 'I wasn't there for you and I'm sorry.'

'You're sorry? You want to spend ten years in this thing.' His friend patted his wheels and grinned. 'What the hell have you got to be sorry for? Yeah, it would have been nice to see your ugly face around a bit more. Or perhaps a few more free tickets. But really…it's okay. I understand.'

'I mean it, man. I should have stopped you. I should have known.'

His friend looked embarrassed, but relieved too. By making a solid effort this wall between them had started to come down slowly, brick by brick. 'I didn't know myself until ten seconds before. I'd been feeling really crap and should have said something. Didn't know where to start. So I thought it'd be easier to finish it.'

'I should have done something though. Seen it coming. And after...I should have been there.'

'Don't beat yourself up about something you had no control over.' Tom lowered his voice. 'I was depressed, okay? I needed my head sorted.'

There was a long pause. Zac looked at Tom. Really looked at him for the first time in years. Saw past the chair and the hurt. Despite everything he was still the same guy he'd known most of his life. The same one he'd joked with, worked with, hell, shared everything with. The years dropped away, melting the anger until they were stripped back to the one thing that held them together—that fragile thread of friendship. Maybe for Tom it had always been there, but Zac had been too scared to look. A stupid ache burnt the back of his throat; he swallowed it away but it wouldn't go. Words were hard to find. 'But I was your mate.'

'Still are?' Tom punched him on his arm.

He punched him back. 'Too right.'

And before he knew it they were laughing and wrapped in a kind of messy scrum. After all those years, the pain in his chest never going away, anger turning to guilt like a hard scar that nothing could ever erase, something in his heart fluttered free. Why hadn't he done something sooner?

'Whoa. Funny look alert.' Zac scanned the smiling faces around them, winced at the wolf whistles and released his mate.

He glanced back at Dani. Couldn't resist one last look. Thank you, he said silently. For the courage to do that.

The camera zoomed in as she strapped Jaxon's ankle, oblivious to the millions watching her in bars and homes around the world. She'd managed to rise above her discomfort of being scrutinised and bore the weight of the team on her shoulders. Zac shook his head. 'I should be there.'

'Mate, after all that trouble you're better off without

them. This way you get to be a fan with the rest of us rather than have the hassle of working.' Tom led the way and ushered him into the packed street. A sea of red, dotted with Samoan blue, flowed ahead towards the stadium. 'And anyway, you've got your new job starting on Monday.'

'I know. But...'

'But what? Spill.' Squeezing the brakes Tom dragged Zac to a quiet part of the pavement away from the music and the cheers. The friend he'd known since college saw what Zac was trying desperately to hide. 'This is about Dani, not the team, right?'

'Yeah.' No use denying it. He'd fallen hard and couldn't let it go.

Tom's eyes narrowed. 'Why her? Why now?'

'After years of dodging the bullet I've...fallen...you know. The L word. I screwed up.'

'Well, give the man a medal. You love her? And you're flying to Melbourne tomorrow? Great timing.'

'Oh, yes. You know me. Master at timing.'

'So what are you going to do?' They edged through the entrance and headed towards their seats.

Yeah...what am I going to do? Doing nothing hadn't worked so far. Maybe he just needed more time. A new job. A new start. 'Go. Forget her.'

The incredulous look in Tom's eyes struck a chord. 'Give up on her? Just like that? That's not like you, Zac. What was our motto? Play hard. Work hard. *Fight* hard.'

'She doesn't want this kind of life. I do. Look at it.' He pointed to the waving flags, the smiling faces, the hyped anxiety of the dedicated fans. 'I love this.'

Tom's eyebrows arched. 'You love a lot of things, Zac. Choose one. Choose her.' Over the roar of cheers as the Samoan team entered the field Tom raised his voice. 'I've watched guilt and grief paralyse you. You filled that hole with work and fundraising, and clung to that as if it was your salvation. Hell knows, I should have said something. But we weren't exactly on good terms. But now…well, I won't stand by and let you ruin your life. I've known you date a lot of women, and none of them have ever made this kind of impression. Are you going to carry on the same old trajectory forever? Or can you allow yourself a chance at something good? How much are you willing to meet Dani halfway? How much are you willing to let go?'

Right now, everything. But that wouldn't work out in the long run. He had a plane to catch, a job to do. And he'd always be doing that. Moving on. Going forward. Being that celebrated successful sports doctor he'd always dreamt about. He couldn't give everything up for her. Could he? 'Jeez, I don't know.'

'Well, I guess you have a handful of hours to work it out.'

Dani finished the last of the strapping and looked at the huddle of players. Final prayers, last team talk and they'd be off. A man from security nodded her way. She hauled in a lungful of air, fisted her hands against her side. Said her own prayer to anyone that might listen. *Please let them win. Let some good come from this.* 'Okay, boys. Time to go.'

The noise in the stadium whipped her breath away; a tremendous cheer echoed across the city as the players ran down the tunnel and out onto the field. Sixty thousand flags of red and blue fluttered in the wind.

The band started up. The anthems. The fearsome war dances. All passed in a haze of tachycardia.

Focus.

But she couldn't settle. A strange prickling awareness tickled the hairs on the back of her neck. She couldn't see him. Not in the thousands of smiling faces. But he was there. She knew it. Watching her. Watching over her.

Somewhere in that crowd was Zac.

For two weeks she'd driven herself to concentrate on her job, to forget the pain of him leaving. Every morning and every night the weight of his absence had pressed in on her until she felt she'd go mad. But work had consumed her waking hours. Made her forget a little of the glorious technicolour she'd felt when with him. She could understand a little now of why he buried himself in his career—it left no space for thinking, hurting.

And now he was here, close by, in the same space she was and she couldn't see his face. How could she be so close to him and not even know where he was?

She'd known she'd miss him. Known it'd take time to get him out of her system. She just hadn't believed it could be so hard. And so slow. She dreamt about his tender touch, his sense of humour. The way his smile lit up her soul. His irritating cockiness that made him all Zac. Pure one hundred percent Zac. Thought she'd seen him in a zillion different faces over the past few days. Prayed she'd catch sight of him one last time before she went back to her life in Wellington.

But now she needed to drag on her big-girl's pants and focus on salvaging at least something.

The whistle blew. Game on.

'Jaxon, what's wrong with you?' She ran onto the field, sponged water over his shoulders to cool him down. 'That's the third time you've gone down with a minor tackle. For goodness sake, get up and run hard. We're losing.'

'I can't. They're targeting me.' The player looked shaken, spooked. She knew how it felt to be in the limelight, to be the one who's blood they wanted. 'Every time I turn round, they're there. In my face.'

'It's what they do. Do it back. I've got Manu off with a shoulder injury. Taylor's in the blood bin, and Marco's done his ACL. This is it, Jaxon. Get up and face them.' Running off she glanced at the stadium clock. Five minutes to half time. Five minutes, then she could have a moment to breathe. To regroup. As if. The whole team was falling apart and she was the only one to fix them up before the final onslaught. They needed to win this. She needed to win this. Her father needed...who cared what her father needed? Damn him for refusing to back down, for making her life so hard. For making Zac leave.

And damn Zac for leaving. Tears pricked her eyes. She scrubbed them away. Damn him for making her feel like this. Like she'd never be whole again.

As she reached the edge of the field a roar went up. Jaxon down again. The faces on the bench shadowed as they all turned to her to sort it out.

Panic gripped her chest. It wasn't a physical fix he needed. Jaxon had to dig deep and find some courage, belief in himself. To dredge every ounce of bravery he could and face the pack. Crikey, if she could do it, then so could he. 'Get up, Jaxon.'

'I can't.'

'Yes, you can. You can do this.' She counted to ten. Looked up at the giant TV screen and saw herself in full view of the world. She turned away, bent down, didn't want everyone to see she was failing. 'Please. I need you to get up.' No, what she needed was a miracle. She needed Zac.

Zac watched as Dani spoke to Jaxon on the field. What she said he didn't know, but he saw the fear flash behind her eyes. The tight thin line of her mouth. The slow journey of her hand to hair. Her hair to her mouth.

If you need anything let me know.

With that single simple action he knew what he was going to do. Knew instantly what she needed.

She needed someone who was as brave as she was, who

wouldn't let the past interfere with the now or the future. She needed someone to love her, to cherish her every day, to hold her close to their heart.

She needed help—and, darn it, whether she liked it or not he was going to give it. Now, and for the rest of her life, if she'd let him.

He hurtled down the stairs, barged along the corridor towards the team changing rooms. Heard the half-time whistle. Slammed up against a burly security guard. 'No, mate. Sorry, only access-all-areas personnel.'

'I'm the Jets doctor. They need me down there.'

Putting his hand on Zac's shoulder the guard flashed a warning smile. 'Yeah, yeah. And I'm the fairy godmother. Right now, I think they need me more.'

Really? A joker? Now? 'You don't understand...'

'Oh, I do, mate. We're all experts at a time like this, I know. But, sorry. You're not going there. Now move along.'

Zac didn't have time to play nicely. Time was running out. He had to get to Dani. He glared past the man, glimpsed a gap behind his bulky frame. Heaved in a breath. One, two, three... In a swift move he dodged to his right, round the man, and sprinted down the corridor.

As he swung open the medical annexe door he gauged Dani's reaction. Saw the brief flutter of her eyelids as if saying a silent thank-you. The small smile on her lips, the questions running through her gaze. All that, in a moment. And more. Saw the love she'd never admitted. The softening of her shoulders. The renewed vigour in her strapping.

And the irritation that infiltrated her smile.

He stepped next to her and started to examine Manu's shoulder. 'You'd better tell security to send off the dogs.'

'I don't need saving. I'm fine.'

He grasped her wrist. 'No, you're not, Dani. Your eyes

were dark out there on the field. You looked panicked. And you were chewing your hair again.'

'It was a *temporary lapse*.' How many times had he heard that? Her perennial excuse for any kind of perceived weakness. She shook her hand free. 'I could have managed without you.'

'I know you could. But isn't it better to accept help every now and then? You don't have to do everything on your own. Come on, you've got to admit you're pleased to see me.'

'Could you get any more self-centred?'

'I doubt it.'

The flashes of irritation softened. 'Okay. Manu can wait a second. I need you to stitch Taylor back together first, then talk to Jaxon.'

'You're the boss.' He moved away, found a suturing kit and began to sew Taylor's head wound, enjoying the hands-on work, but the eyes-on Dani more. His heart thumped a weird rhythm as he looked at her. Had he ever told her how beautiful she was? How much she made his day just by being close. He was going to tell her that every day. Starting now. Well, starting after the game. He was going to woo her, court her, make love to her. Take her on dates, go at her pace. Wherever she wanted to be.

She peered over his shoulder at his handiwork and he reeled at the exotic scent that made his head whirl. The aroma that had become ingrained in his clothes, his brain. That he didn't think he'd ever get to smell again. 'Nice stitches, Doc.'

'Thank you. Now, Jaxon.'

She pulled him aside. 'He's delicate. Feeling the pressure and a little highly strung. I need you to be firm but gentle. Empathetic, but assertive. You get the picture?'

He pressed his hand to her cheek. 'When do I get to kiss you?'

'What?' Her mouth twitched. She glanced towards her father, who stood in the corner of the room watching them.

Zac laughed. Hell, he was already in big trouble with security, he might as well upset the whole darned fun police. 'At what point do I get to kiss you?'

But she moved his hand away. Let it drop by his side. 'This is so inappropriate. We're running out of time.'

'Start as you mean to go on, I say.'

'Patients. Win. Talk…I mean, really talk, Zac. Then… whatever…' She ticked them off on her fingers. 'In that order, you hear? We have two more minutes before the next half.'

'Aye, aye. But I'm looking forward to…*whatever*.' He saluted and went to find Jaxon. He was sitting apart from the other players, his head in his hands. 'Jaxon, you okay?'

'No. Not really.' The kid's eyes were haunted and dark.

'I know this is massive pressure. But you'll do fine. They're hitting you because you're the best. They want you to go down, to break your resolve. But you're faster, lighter, smarter. Yeah?'

'Yeah.' Jaxon nodded, but looked far from convinced.

'Get round them.'

'I can't.'

'Think, Jaxon. Think back to those boys in the wheelchairs. Do they worry about what they can't do? Do they feel sorry for themselves? No. So you've got to think about what you *can* do. You know you can beat them. You know you can outwit them. You can do this. Believe it.'

'I don't know…' But his shoulders had straightened a bit. Fire smouldered behind his eyes.

'Take the hits. Take a risk. You can do anything you want, you've just got to want it badly enough. This is your time, Jaxon. Reach out and take it. Don't look back in years to come and wish you'd grasped what you wanted.' It all became clear now. This speech wasn't just about Jaxon, it was about himself. He wanted Dani and was going to do whatever it took to get her back. 'Now get out there and win this damned game for the boys at Treetops. You have one chance. Don't stuff it up.'

He ushered Jaxon out with the rest of the players, hoping he'd talked some sense into him, then grabbed Dani's hand. 'Come on, it's starting.'

Don't look back in years to come and wish you'd grasped what you wanted. Dani saw the passion in Zac's eyes. Did he believe that? And if he did, why had he walked away?

Why had he come back?

She dropped his hand immediately despite her fingers automatically curling into his. Drew herself away and walked down the tunnel alone onto the side of the pitch. Sure, he'd come back. But for what? More kisses? More meaningless fun? She couldn't let herself get carried away with hope.

'I can't believe this is happening.' Zac leaned into her as they sat at the end of the bench, another thirty-nine minutes of torture later. An uncertain silence hovered round the stadium. Jaxon stepped up to kick the ball. This was their last chance to secure the dream. One kick. Three points. One delighted Davide. Millions of happy people.

So much was riding on this. She couldn't help but cling to Zac's jacket, hold her breath. Watch Jaxon's face. He glanced over to the bench and nodded.

Zac nodded back. Jaxon stepped up to kick. The ball soared towards the post. The whistle blew.

Then Zac's arms were round her waist. His nose pressed against hers. 'He scored! We won. My God, we won!'

She felt herself being lifted and swirled round. Heard the fuzzy noise of the crowd. Everything appeared to be in slow motion, the waving arms of sixty thousand people, the screaming players, the rising elation of being in his arms again.

As he lowered her to the ground Zac gazed at her. His mouth hitched into a smile as he tilted her chin. His eyes emanated such warmth it was hard not to be mesmerised by them. 'I love you, Daniella Danatello.'

Oh. Not what she expected. She didn't want it to be true, not unless he meant it with his heart and soul. 'No, you don't, you love the Jets. You love winning.'

'Sure, I love that too.' He nodded. 'But most of all, I love you, Dani.'

Her chest tightened, her throat tightened. Her hand shook as she pressed it to her mouth. 'Please don't say it if you don't mean it. I couldn't bear it if you woke up tomorrow and realised you'd got carried away in the moment.'

'I mean it with every part of my being. I've spent the past two weeks not knowing what I was doing, going round in a daze. I missed you so much and realised I was a coward to walk away from something so special. But I was scared. Scared of giving, of loving again. But I hurt, Dani. A part of me was actually in pain when I wasn't with you. I don't want to feel like that again. Please tell me you feel the same.'

She gasped, laughed. Cried. 'I...don't know what to say.'

'I know I'm going out on a limb here, but you could say you love me too.'

'Yes. Yes, of course, you idiot. I love you too.'

'Excellent.' Then he began to lower to one knee, in front of all those cheering people, the cameras, her father. Damn her father. Damn the crowd. 'I know this isn't the best place to do this. I'm sure you'd like it in a more private place, but I want to do it right now. Right. Now. Just so you don't think any of this is a *temporary lapse*. And I'm guessing everyone's looking at the players celebrating on the pitch, not at me. Doing this.'

'Oh, my goodness.' She grabbed his shoulder, tried to hitch him up. Still not believing he could mean it. 'What about your job? My job. Our lives? We need to talk about things.'

'I know if you love me like I love you we'll work it out. If that means moving to Wellington, I'll do it. Or you could come to Melbourne. Or we could meet in the middle somewhere.'

'The ocean? Like that would work.'

'I'm trying to compromise here. It's a new concept… work with me a little. Whatever you want. You are the funniest, sexiest woman I've ever met and I'm totally lost without you.' He shrugged and tried to stand, but she pushed him back down.

'But what about your big-shot sports doctor dream?'

'Will you quit with the questions?' He grimaced and pointed to his bended knee. 'This is starting to hurt. *This* is my dream. You and me.'

'And Treetops?'

He grew serious, ran his thumb over the back of her hand. 'I don't want it to be a burden, but yes, take me, take Treetops.'

She looked at him half standing, half kneeling, with love burning in his eyes and knew she'd take whatever he offered. He wanted to spend his life with her. Treetops could be nothing but an additional joy. 'Burden? Never. I'd love to help.'

'Then, marry me?'

She pulled him to face her. Managed to squeeze the words out. 'Yes, of course. Yes.'

'Thank God.' He whispered as he closed in, 'And we have two thousand condoms to make a start on.'

'Of course! The tournament's over. No more sex-free

sex.' She snagged his shoulder, imagining what fun they could have. 'Do you have a one-track mind?'

'With you? Hell, yes.'

His arms circled her waist as he drew her to him, pressed his mouth on hers and clung to her as if he would never let her go. And she clung right on back, peace and excitement, joy and hope, rolling through her.

As if on cue, tiny pieces of white ticker-tape began to flutter down onto their heads, covering their shoulders like confetti. Another loud roar rumbled through the crowd like a Mexican wave, louder and louder until the whole stadium rang with the sound of cheers and clapping and stamping of feet.

'They must be lifting the trophy.'

'Oh. That.' He rested his forehead against hers and they turned to face the screen. 'No. It's us. They're cheering for us.'

Daniella felt the sudden rush of blood to her cheeks as she saw a huge picture of herself, laughing in Zac's arms, beamed out across the globe. Into the homes of millions of people, and no doubt straight onto tomorrow's front pages. And for once she didn't care. Just ached for another kiss. Then another. And another…

Breaking News…
Lady Godiva Marries Sir Love-a-Lot

The News Women's Page *can finally confirm that the rumour mill is correct. After their very public display of affection following the Jets' dramatic win of the Pan Asia Pacific Tournament six months ago, Dani Danatello and her fiancé, Zachary Price, allegedly married earlier today in a private ceremony.*
Sources close to the couple report that the nuptials

took place at Zac's holiday home in North Beach, north of Auckland, during a break away from his job at the Wellington Blues. A marquee was erected in the substantial garden and a local flower delivery company were overheard to comment that they have been particularly busy for the past few days. Dani's sisters and father, entrepreneur Davide Danatello, are rumoured to be staying at the Castle, a local boutique luxury lodge close to North Beach. Zac's father and mother, Marguerite and Rufus Price, have also recently been seen hiking the extensive ranges in the vicinity.

Honeymoon details have been kept under wraps. But our sources report that a bright yellow campervan left the venue at three o'clock and was last seen heading south.

* * * * *

Mills & Boon® Hardback
April 2013

ROMANCE

Master of her Virtue	Miranda Lee
The Cost of her Innocence	Jacqueline Baird
A Taste of the Forbidden	Carole Mortimer
Count Valieri's Prisoner	Sara Craven
The Merciless Travis Wilde	Sandra Marton
A Game with One Winner	Lynn Raye Harris
Heir to a Desert Legacy	Maisey Yates
The Sinful Art of Revenge	Maya Blake
Marriage in Name Only?	Anne Oliver
Waking Up Married	Mira Lyn Kelly
Sparks Fly with the Billionaire	Marion Lennox
A Daddy for Her Sons	Raye Morgan
Along Came Twins...	Rebecca Winters
An Accidental Family	Ami Weaver
A Date with a Bollywood Star	Riya Lakhani
The Proposal Plan	Charlotte Phillips
Their Most Forbidden Fling	Melanie Milburne
The Last Doctor She Should Ever Date	Louisa George

MEDICAL

NYC Angels: Unmasking Dr Serious	Laura Iding
NYC Angels: The Wallflower's Secret	Susan Carlisle
Cinderella of Harley Street	Anne Fraser
You, Me and a Family	Sue MacKay

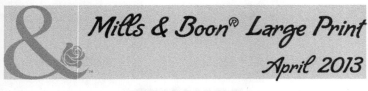

Mills & Boon® Large Print
April 2013

ROMANCE

A Ring to Secure His Heir	Lynne Graham
What His Money Can't Hide	Maggie Cox
Woman in a Sheikh's World	Sarah Morgan
At Dante's Service	Chantelle Shaw
The English Lord's Secret Son	Margaret Way
The Secret That Changed Everything	Lucy Gordon
The Cattleman's Special Delivery	Barbara Hannay
Her Man in Manhattan	Trish Wylie
At His Majesty's Request	Maisey Yates
Breaking the Greek's Rules	Anne McAllister
The Ruthless Caleb Wilde	Sandra Marton

HISTORICAL

Some Like It Wicked	Carole Mortimer
Born to Scandal	Diane Gaston
Beneath the Major's Scars	Sarah Mallory
Warriors in Winter	Michelle Willingham
A Stranger's Touch	Anne Herries

MEDICAL

A Socialite's Christmas Wish	Lucy Clark
Redeeming Dr Riccardi	Leah Martyn
The Family Who Made Him Whole	Jennifer Taylor
The Doctor Meets Her Match	Annie Claydon
The Doctor's Lost-and-Found Heart	Dianne Drake
The Man Who Wouldn't Marry	Tina Beckett

0313 GEN STD LP

Mills & Boon® Hardback

May 2013

ROMANCE

A Rich Man's Whim	Lynne Graham
A Price Worth Paying?	Trish Morey
A Touch of Notoriety	Carole Mortimer
The Secret Casella Baby	Cathy Williams
Maid for Montero	Kim Lawrence
Captive in his Castle	Chantelle Shaw
Heir to a Dark Inheritance	Maisey Yates
A Legacy of Secrets	Carol Marinelli
Her Deal with the Devil	Nicola Marsh
One More Sleepless Night	Lucy King
A Father for Her Triplets	Susan Meier
The Matchmaker's Happy Ending	Shirley Jump
Second Chance with the Rebel	Cara Colter
First Comes Baby...	Michelle Douglas
Anything but Vanilla...	Liz Fielding
It was Only a Kiss	Joss Wood
Return of the Rebel Doctor	Joanna Neil
One Baby Step at a Time	Meredith Webber

MEDICAL

NYC Angels: Flirting with Danger	Tina Beckett
NYC Angels: Tempting Nurse Scarlet	Wendy S. Marcus
One Life Changing Moment	Lucy Clark
P.S. You're a Daddy!	Dianne Drake

Mills & Boon® Large Print
May 2013

ROMANCE

Beholden to the Throne	Carol Marinelli
The Petrelli Heir	Kim Lawrence
Her Little White Lie	Maisey Yates
Her Shameful Secret	Susanna Carr
The Incorrigible Playboy	Emma Darcy
No Longer Forbidden?	Dani Collins
The Enigmatic Greek	Catherine George
The Heir's Proposal	Raye Morgan
The Soldier's Sweetheart	Soraya Lane
The Billionaire's Fair Lady	Barbara Wallace
A Bride for the Maverick Millionaire	Marion Lennox

HISTORICAL

Some Like to Shock	Carole Mortimer
Forbidden Jewel of India	Louise Allen
The Caged Countess	Joanna Fulford
Captive of the Border Lord	Blythe Gifford
Behind the Rake's Wicked Wager	Sarah Mallory

MEDICAL

Maybe This Christmas...?	Alison Roberts
A Doctor, A Fling & A Wedding Ring	Fiona McArthur
Dr Chandler's Sleeping Beauty	Melanie Milburne
Her Christmas Eve Diamond	Scarlet Wilson
Newborn Baby For Christmas	Fiona Lowe
The War Hero's Locked-Away Heart	Louisa George

0413 GEN STD LP